THE FATAL MOVE

The Fatal Move

by

Conall Cearnach

Swan River Press
Dublin, Ireland
MMXXIV

The Fatal Move
by Conall Cearnach

Published by
Swan River Press
at Æon House
Dublin, Ireland
June MMXXIV

www.swanriverpress.ie
brian@swanriverpress.ie

Introduction © Reggie Chamberlain-King
This edition © Swan River Press

Cover design by Meggan Kehrli
from artwork by Thomas Grogan (1923)

Set in Garamond by Ken Mackenzie

Paperback Edition
ISBN 978-1-78380-779-6

Swan River Press published
a limited hardback edition of
The Fatal Move in April 2021.

Contents

Selected Essays

F. W. O'Connell:
Master of Strange Tongues

I.

Recalled more as a man of languages than as a man of letters, Frederick William O'Connell (known widely by the pseudonym "Conall Cearnach") was a scholar and polyglot who took a strange delight in the intermingling of his own and other cultures. As a translator, he took a keen interest in the fantastical and magical, while, in his own weird writing, he was influenced by the many faiths, languages, and practices he explored in his academic work. "There were few scholars in Ireland," a commentator wrote in the *Irish Times*, "who could rival him as a linguist: for he was a master of strange tongues" (21 October 1929). Predominantly an Irish-speaker and author of *A Grammar of Old Irish* (1912) and *Irish Self-Taught* (1923), as well as three volumes of essays—*The Writings on the Walls* (1915), *The Age of Whitewash* (1921), and *Old Wine & New* (1922)—his international interests make his a uniquely generous conception of Irishness.

The Fatal Move and Other Stories represents O'Connell's only published collection of fiction. It is a slender volume of fantastical writing, with no fixed centre: like the author himself, the book displays diverse interests, looking far back into the past and considering possible variants of the future. The book was published for the Christmas market in 1923 (though it is given as "1924" on the title page), when a recently-partitioned Ireland was fighting over the past and contending with dual futures itself. If the book is disjointed, so were the times.

O'Connell occupied an unusual position in those times too. He was a native *Gaeilgeoir* (Irish-speaker) from the rural west, but a Protestant divine who flourished in the industrial Unionist north. His nationalism was soft and welcoming, but his satire was sharp and needling. He was a respected member of the community in both capital cities, Belfast and Dublin, and occupied high seats in institutions on either side of the border. By the time he died, he was, in the words of Aodh de Blacam, "among the most popular figures in contemporary Dublin and not less so because of his great modesty". The weird scenes that accompanied his tragic death would have embarrassed him had he witnessed them, but they too show how he embodied many contradictions expressive of the time.

This edition of *The Fatal Move* is the first time the book has been reprinted in the almost hundred years since it was first published, and this introduction represents one of the few extensive overviews of the author's life.

Like many Irish writers before him, O'Connell was the Anglican clergyman son of an Anglican clergyman. His mother was Catherine Eleanor Donnelly; his father, the Rev. William Morgan O'Connell, rector of Omey and Clifden, Co. Galway, in the Diocese of Tuam, Killala, and Achonry. Frederick was born there on 22 October 1876. On the 1911 census, Catherine is recorded as having given birth to two children, of which one—Frederick—was still living.

The life of a clergyman or a clergyman's child can be turbulent, frequently migrating from parish to parish. However, in childhood at least, O'Connell was well-grounded in Clifden, the coastal town considered the unofficial capital of Connemara in the province of Connaught. That part of western Ireland contains the largest proportion of native Irish speakers. Even in the present day, approximately 20,000 of Connemara's 32,000 inhabitants are native Irish speakers. It was in this unique and self-sustaining environment that Frederick O'Connell grew up and, even as member of the Church of Ireland, he was raised in the Irish language and with the customs of the rural "Wild West".

The town was founded in the early nineteenth century by John D'Arcy of Kiltullagh parish and the barony of Athenry, and it saw brief prosperity as a harbour town shipping Connemara marble. However, the devastation of the famine of 1845 halted the town's growth. By 1848, ninety per cent of the town's population were receiving government relief and many emigrated. John D'Arcy's heir—Hyacinth D'Arcy—sold his father's failing estates in 1850 to absentee landlord brothers Charles and Thomas Eyre. He retreated into the life of an Anglican clergyman, becoming the rector of Omey and Clifden.

In his forties, William Morgan O'Connell chose to do the same and was ordained in 1892. He began as curate in Drumshanbo, then canon in Drumreilly, both Co. Leitrim, before taking up a post at Aasleagh, in the Erriff Valley, Co. Mayo, where he and his wife lived for many years caring for his mother-in-law. He eventually became rector of Omey and Clifden, like Hyacinth D'Arcy, taking on the additional responsibilities of the Rural Dean of Galway from 1907 to 1916, Prebendary of Kilmainmore in Tuam Cathedral, Galway from 1925, Precentor of Tuam from 1925 to 1928, and Rural Dean of Tuam from 1944.

At the same time, Frederick had been accepted to Trinity College Dublin via a series of entrance prizes in both modern and ancient languages, which he won while attending the High School in Dublin. This was the same school in Rathgar where W. B. Yeats had been schooled a decade earlier. Among O'Connell's contemporaries was James Cousins (1873-1956), the Belfast-born theosophist, playwright, and orientalist. O'Connell obtained an Honours B.A. in Modern Literature in 1900. While at the university, he and several other divinity students founded the Druidical Society, with, in the words of fellow Druid, J. B. Shea, "Cearnach as chief druid". Together, they published the short-lived college newspaper, *An tEorpach*: "perhaps the most singular paper hitherto published within these islands, inasmuch as it found place for every language but English". O'Connell was able to contribute copy in Japanese, Russian, French, Italian, and German, for a start.

In 1902, eleven years after his father, O'Connell was ordained in the Church of Ireland. He took a Bachelor of Divinity degree in 1905 and an M.A. in 1908, then the fellowship prizeman in Classical and Semitic Philology.

His first post was as curate of Newtownforbes, Co. Longford, then, following in his father's footsteps again, he became curate-in-charge of Drumshanbo, Co. Leitrim. He married Helen (*née* Young, of Nenagh Co. Tipperary) in 1904, and they had two sons, in 1907 and 1909, when he was rector of Castleconnor and Achonry, Co. Sligo. In 1909, he moved to Belfast, where he was granted a general licence from the Bishop of the united dioceses of Down, Connor, and Dromore. This allowed him to preach at any parish within the dioceses—or not to preach, whichever was the more agreeable.

In 1905, Marconi built his first long-wave wireless telegraphy station at Clifden—though O'Connell would point out that the word should be "telegraphema". But, even in comparison to this modern development, Belfast was a very different world. The most prosperous city in Ireland, it was the site of one of the world's most important shipyards, where construction of the *Titanic* was underway, as well as linen works and rope works that serviced the British Empire.

The culture was also different. The people of Ulster were predominantly Protestant—largely Presbyterian—and political power there rested with the Ulster Unionist Council, founded in 1905, which would fight against the threat of Home Rule. Influence was channelled through the tributaries of fraternal institutions: the Orange Order; elite schools such as Royal Belfast Academical Institution ("Inst."), Campbell College, and Belfast Royal Academy; and an "old boys" network emanating from Queen's University.

It was that institute which brought and kept O'Connell in Belfast. After completing his M.A., he became lecturer of Celtic Languages and Literatures there. It was the first position of its kind at the university and bore the political weight of being an offering to the city's Catholic minority, as the Irish language was heavily politicised.

But to O'Connell, the attitude to the Irish language of many Irish Protestants, especially in the North, was, as he argued in his essay "Patriotism and Language" (*The Writings on the Walls*), "utterly senseless, illogical and inconsistent". He continued: "In my opinion, the national language is the birthright of every Irishman, independent of creed or politics, and to say we [Irish Protestants] should have nothing to do with the Irish language because it is spoken principally by Catholics and Nationalists is as sensible as though I refused to go on a tramcar and took 'Shank's mare' because the majority of tram conductors were Orangemen. If it is a question of religion, let them be consistent, let them eschew Latin, for it is the language of 'Popery'."

Although a champion of the Irish language, O'Connell's career as an Anglican minister and his non-politicised sense of national identity made him a palatable candidate for the school's Protestant administration. As a learned linguist, he was able to place the Irish language—and its attendant customs, traditions, mindsets, and mythologies—in a global context, which elevated it above immediate party political concerns. He threw himself into the role with vigour and, even when the university senate turned down a call to turn the lectureship into a university chair, O'Connell continued. Regardless of their decision, the university paid him a full professor's salary for a lecturer's role.

Belfast was a good home for an eccentric Anglican like O'Connell. The university allowed him opportunity for research and the city had an open and vibrant literary culture. The family lived at 66 University Square, in the Botanic area of the city, minutes from the university and the home of Herbert Moore Pim (1883-1950), another unconventional Protestant nationalist and writer of fantastical fiction. This kept them far from much of the unrest that would take place in the city in the 1910s and '20s. Fittingly, the building a few doors down would become International House, Northern Ireland's leading institute for teaching English as a foreign language.

As an outsider who was allowed inside, he developed a genuine affection for the city. While others used the term with an aggrandising seriousness, when O'Connell called Belfast the "Athens of the North" he did so with the satirist's smirk. Yes, Belfast, like Athens, was a city of prosperity, of politics, and poetics, but it was also a classical city state—that is, a city on its own, with its own culture, its own way of doing things, which could not necessarily be woven into the fabric of a new nation.

In "The Writing on the Wall", he compared it to another city of antiquity: "If Cave Hill suddenly became an active volcano, and buried the city of Belfast under sixty feet of ashes, the excavators of 2915 AD would find that however much it differed from Pompeii in such matters as architecture and water supply, the street scribblings of both cities had much in common." The political graffiti that covered the gable-ends of his adopted city, although more prone to swearing, represented similar concerns to those of our classical forebears: representation, identity, shared allegiance. Many politically-motivated outrages took place in Belfast while O'Connell lived there, but while the intense heat of these moments lasted only a moment, there were universal human experiences that would resonate forever: "If the eruption of Ben Madigan should take place, and Macaulay's New Zealander should . . . stroll through the excavated ruins of Belfast, he would find human nature in such wall-scribblings as: 'J— is in love with M—' and 'Tom S— is an ass'; but what would he make of . . . 'Remember 1690!', 'Votes for Women' and above all 'To H— with the P—'?"

This was the lens through which he saw everything: the ancient, the mythic, poetic, and folkloric. There was nothing new under the sun and nothing new in human experience—he looked for the things that united us. And, when humans were being silly, he would respond in kind. As Ireland faced partition, he sought a workable solution not in the immediate future, but in the ancient past. In the essay, "A Moral from Man" (*The Age of Whitewash*), he noted that our Manx brethren avoided accusations of impartiality in their venerable justice system by having the court sit on a mound artificially created from a mixture of soils from each quarterland on the island—no judgment could be said to have been made on partisan earth. Modern Ireland already has such a place, at the mounds of Tara, if we could only look past fourteen centuries of inconsequential politics: "a new Convocation of Tara might avoid even the semblance of Partition and the men of Erin find peace and prosperity".

O'Connell worked in Belfast for sixteen years. He and Helen had two more children there: Maurice and Eileen. They later moved to the Seacliff Road, on the seafront at Bangor, Co. Down. It is reputed that he was physically assaulted for speaking Irish along the Bangor promenade, but that did not diminish his affection for the place. It was only when his wife, Helen, died of tuberculosis in 1925 that he left Northern

Ireland. It was in Ulster that he concentrated his focus on writing, especially his interest in weird and unusual works.

He began in 1909 with a translation of Brian Mac Giolla Meidhre's *Cúirt An Mhean Oíche*, the great Irish comic poem of the Fairy Queen's arbitration over human women's sexual mistreatment by men. O'Connell's version of the erotic romp, *The Midnight Court* (1909), was published as a school's edition several decades before Frank O'Connor's more famous translation was banned in Ireland. Flann O'Brien (1911-1966), in his "Cruiskeen Lawn" column in the *Irish Times* (written under the pseudonym "Myles na gCopaleen"), reminded readers of the translation by his "old friend and former student, Conall Cearnach". Given that O'Brien was eighteen years old when O'Connell died, this might be a wry reference to the latter's profile as an educator.

The Midnight Court was followed by translations of Geoffrey Keating's *Giotaí as Trí bior-ghaoithe an bháis* (*The Three Shafts of Death*) in 1910 and, in 1915, *An Irish corpus astronomiae: being Manus O'Donnell's seventeenth century version of the Lunario of Geronymo Cortès*. Translating from English into Irish, he assisted Peadar Ó Laoghaire with his translation of Cervantes's *Don Cíochóte* (1921); O'Connell produced also the first Irish translation of Robert Louis Stevenson's *Cás aduain an Dr Jekyll agus Mhr Hyde* (1929).

The latter was a personal favourite of O'Connell, which he considered "the most thrilling story that Stevenson ever penned" and a "pure tragedy" of man divided against himself. O'Connell was horrified by the 1913 film adaptation of the tale by Carl Laemmle's Independent Moving Pictures, which foregrounded Jekyll's romantic entanglements, turning "pure tragedy" into "melodrama". It was "obviously the production of an American company. One could feel that Dr. Jekyll was really Dr. Wm. L. Jekyll and Hyde—surely Elihu P. Hyde—was returning from a 'bust' in the Bowery" ("The

Cinematograph", *The Writings on the Walls*). The film was, in fact, the work of the Irish director, Herbert Brenon (1880-1958), working in California.

O'Connell clearly saw something deeper in Stevenson's then forty-year-old story that could be illuminated through translation into Irish (and, therefore into an Irish context). By 1929 the island of Ireland had been partitioned for almost a decade. The War of Independence and the Civil War had caused ruination in the Irish Free State—in the tired way of civil wars everywhere, brother had been set against brother, even in Clifden. In Northern Ireland, the troubled twenties saw street violence and pogroms against the Catholic minority—mild-mannered neighbours were subsumed into violent mobs. The political union of which Ireland had been part failed to accommodate duality and the result was a murderous breaking in two.

The Irish language represented, for O'Connell, the birth-right of all Irish people, a source of national identity that long predated the petty divisions of religion and politics. He saw, in it and the ancient history associated with it, an identity that could accommodate the dualities in the hearts of his countrymen. Perhaps the academic exercise of translating *Strange Case of Dr. Jekyll and Mr. Hyde* into the national language was a symbolic act of unification.

Significantly, the translation was published under a pen-name, "Conall Cearnach", a play on O'Connell's own surname and the hero of the Ulster Cycle. In mythology, the Ulsterman, Conall Cearnach, engaged in a bloody feud with his uncle, the Connaughtman, Cet mac Mágach, and it was prophesied that he would kill half the men of Connaught. It was typical of O'Connell's humour to mythologise in himself a conflict between the province from whence he came and the province in which he thrived. The name encoded some of the dualities in O'Connell's identity as a writer: Anglican, but *Gaeilgeoir*, contemporary, but ancient; Ulsterman, but Connaughtman; and, therefore, an Irishman.

He first adopted the pseudonym in 1915, when he embarked on a parallel career as an essayist. He published with M. H. Gill & Son in Dublin three collections of essays in English: *The Writings on the Walls* (1915), *The Age of Whitewash* (1921), and *Old Wine and New* (1922).

It is through the essays that we get the clearest idea of O'Connell as a person. He covers a wide range of subjects, from the insignificant to the timeless, matching an interest in the contemporaneous with the archaic. He wrote about the cinematograph and prohibition with the same brio as he did the Oxyrhynchus Papyri and old Gaelic hygiene. It was all the same to him. From any starting point, he could work his way back to one of his many interests or pet theories. To an extent, it was a game to see where he could end up from whence he began. Per a review in the *Irish Weekly*, he had "a faculty of observation combined with a genius for memorising what is worth mental retention" (*The Advocate*, 20 July 1922). He was a landmine of useless information.

Although he was prone to prodding ("full of measured, constructive satire and sarcasm"), there was little fight in him: his snark was worse than his bite. "He is the sort of man it would be a perfect delight to disagree with," wrote the *Freeman's Journal*; "A reader may dissent from Conall Cearnach in many of his conclusions; but no reader could possibly fail to be entertained and even unconsciously educated and made sensible of the best within him through mere association with such a delightful companion" (14 September 1922).

Ireland, of course, took prominence in his writing, but it was an outward-looking Irishness. He spoke with pride of meeting Irishmen in every country and city he visited. In one essay collected in *The Writings on the Walls*, he sets out his theory that Irish is the "Master Key to all Linguistics" (a thread tugged at a little later by Umberto Eco) and, in many others, he hops between Ireland, Asia, and the Middle East as though they all represent fragments of the whole called Humanity. It is with a similar ease that he references Bergson or his wide reading in psychology, the Bard, or the Vedic hymns. And yet the whole is unified by a certain quality.

The venerated Australian critic, P. I. O'Leary identified this quality thusly: "[Cearnach] is one of the half-dozen living writers in English who can write an essay. He has all the qualities—lightness of touch, urbanity, sweetness, and that extremely rare gift of adding in with his admixture of beauty just a little strangeness" (*The Advocate*, 20 July 1922). The occasional strangeness, with his detours into dreams, juggling, sun worship, and other curious avenues, may explain why O'Connell's name has not lasted like other essayists, fellow Ulsterman Robert Lynd for example. In the eyes of O'Leary, at least, he stood among them. In an article decrying the state of the Australian essay, the writer asked "Why then have we not our Beerbohms . . . our very own Conall Cearnachs, Chestertons, Lucases, Lambs, and Lynds?" Chesterton himself noted *Old Wine and New* "an interesting little book", and seemed persuaded by the theory, in the essay "Cuchulainn and America", that the American continent had been visited by Irish missionaries in the Dark Ages. Although Cearnach's sarcastic conclusion to the piece suggests the author didn't take it quite as seriously.

O'Connell is unlikely to have taken O'Leary's comparison seriously; he was, of course, a man of "great modesty". However, the comparison does make some sense of his one collection of weird fiction. The renowned essayists of the time made their own excursions into fiction and, if one considers the output of Chesterton, Wells, and Shaw, they were all too willing to follow a bent toward the fantastical. These were writers for whom ideas—although pertaining to serious real world conditions—were playthings. What difference was there to explore them in an imaginative essay versus an imaginative story? The books of essays and *The Fatal Move* were all released under the same pseudonym and, to an extent, they cover the same territory.

II.

The Fatal Move contains six varied and variable stories, ranging from the darkly macabre, to the speculative, to the absurd. They represent a similar range in subject to his other writing: the past, the future; Ireland, the world; the strange and the sarcastic. It is a little book and, according to one review, "pity 'tis that 'tis so little" (*Studies*, March 1924).

The title story is a *conte cruel* in which two chess obsessed Frenchmen turn a game into a match to the death. Régnaud and Dubert have long competed for the affections of the widow, Jeannette, and to settle the dispute, Régnaud devises an electrified board with the capacity to kill one player or the other. Neither man can know which move is fatal—murder or suicide—until he makes it.

"To say that 'The Fatal Move'," wrote O'Leary, "is not unworthy of a place beside Poe's 'The Cask of Amontillado' is not to overpraise a remarkable piece of work." The story shares a brutality with Poe's tale of sociopathic revenge and is in a tradition of tales in which duelling goes wrong. There are examples written by fellow Irishmen: "The Dualitists" (1886) by Bram Stoker and Mervyn Wall's "The Men Who Could Outstare Cobras" (1966). The idea of a prototype chess machine that deals out cold-blooded death was previously explored in Ambrose Bierce's story "Moxon's Master" (1899).

However, Cearnach needn't have been a student of the macabre to envisage such barbarism. The events of the story take place in the aftermath of the recently-ended Great

War, a conflict that saw the mechanisation of death on an unimaginable scale. Indeed, Jeannette, the object of the men's interest, is only now widowed and available to them because of the atrocities of that war. Desensitised by four years of violence, a suicidal chess machine may appear a completely rational way to resolve a feud between friends.

True to himself, Cearnach introduces his homeland into proceedings. Régnaud is owner of a set of ancient bronze Irish chessmen and "It was the ancient Irish chessman that gave me the idea" to build the death machine. There is little doubt that the author saw the brinkmanship in Ireland as a game in which the players were willing to cause themselves the greatest harm in order to "win". Such timeliness may explain why "The Fatal Move" provided the title of the collection over some of the better stories in the book.

The story also provided inspiration for the *art nouveau* cover depicted on both the 1924 edition and the current volume. The gorgeous green ink image on a tan background shows the two wearied players slumped on their chess board, watched by the giant face of an Edwardian beauty—presumably the widow Jeannette. Little is known of the cover artist, and until recently even his name had been lost to time. A first edition copy of *The Fatal Move*, now in the Swan River Press archives, bears two inscriptions. The first: "To the Artist with the Publisher's Compliments, Dec. 1923"; the second: "From Tom Grogan, as a specimen of his productions, *le hárd-cion* [with great affection]". Using the same red ink as he had for the second inscription, the artist took the liberty of enlivening Jeannette's eyes on the cover with scarlet pupils. However, the identity of Tom Grogan still remains a mystery. A "Father Thomas Grogan" was registered at the Dublin Metropolitan School of Art in 1919 and seems a possible candidate. One review of *Old Wine and New* spoke of O'Connell "veil[ing] a priestly life and priestly learning under a pseudonym".

It is possible that he would have priestly friends working in other fields too. As a tip of the hat to the Tom Grogan, we have decided to retain the artist's embellishment for the cover of this edition.

The second story in the collection, "The Vengeance of the Dead", is tarnished by racist stereotypes, as two Trinity College students, a Hindu and a Muslim, engage in aggressive practical jokes via occult means. When one of the adversaries dies, the rivalry continues from beyond the grave.

Nevertheless, the story is still of interest, when one grants Cearnach his cock-eyed wit. Chatterjee, the central character, is "by no means an orthodox Hindoo", as he is more influenced by Arya Samaj (a contemporary reform movement) and Annie Besant, the Theosophist thinker and advocate for Irish and Indian independence. In this way, Cearnach subverts the convention of the mystic Easterner. Indeed, while the protagonist of the weird story is frequently enamoured of esoteric practices and substances from the exotic East, here an Indian man is seduced by the American practice of spiritualism and possibly duped by a shady American medium.

Of all the stories, the narrator here seems most closely to resemble O'Connell himself: a wry Irish collegeman who is Chatterjee's critic and confidante. It feels safe to assume that the scepticism expressed represents O'Connell's own view of spiritualism and that he is engaging in his gentle satire once again. It is typical that he would place a person of colour at the centre of a practice that habitually permitted them as spirit guides: the Persian princes, Native American chiefs, and Indian royalty that spoke through mediums, mere figments of white Anglo-American imaginations.

O'Connell certainly would not have been unaccustomed to the sectarian animus that charges the story. By showing Chatterjee as an unorthodox Hindu locked in a battle with the devout Muslim, Ali, he highlights the true nature of such conflicts. They are not really religious or political disputes, as Chatterjee does not represent the conventional man of his faith or nation. Rather, they are cultural, historical, and psychological divisions, long-held and invested in symbols and artefacts, and fully occupying the minds of those who perpetuate them. Even death can't bring an end to it. From the outside, the enmity between Chatterjee and Ali seems silly and petty, but which of Cearnach's Irish readers took their own pettiness as seriously?

Another interesting possibility is that the characters here might represent an affectionate portrait of O'Connell's friend and teacher, Professor Mir Aulad Ali. In fact, J. B. Shea, in a letter to the *Irish Times*, confirms that O'Connell "was the favourite pupil of Mir Aulad Ali" (17 November 1947). Originally from Oudh in the Mughal Empire, Mir Aulad spent forty years as professor of Arabic, Hindustani, and Persian in Trinity College Dublin, where he taught Indian Civil Service students, such as the narrator of "The Vengeance of the Dead", and those with an interest in Oriental languages, such as O'Connell. He was a *Gaeilgeoir* and member of Conradh na Gaeilge (successor to the Gaelic Union). Beloved in the university community, he would frequently make social appearances in the outfit attributed to Chatterjee in O'Connell's story, although Mir Aulad was himself a Muslim. The professor makes several appearances in O'Connell's essays and was an influential figure on both A.E. and James Joyce. Most relevant to "The Vengeance of the Dead" is a memory that Yeats recorded in *Reveries Over Childhood and Youth* (1915), in which Mir Aulad saw "a vision in a pool of ink, a multitude of spirits singing in Arabic", which is reminiscent of the vision of the Taj in a glass of water that Chatterjee shares with the narrator as the foundation of his faith in spiritualism.

The most successful story in the collection is "The Fiend That Walks Behind". Evoking the same supernatural menace found in the tales of Joseph Sheridan Le Fanu, this story unravels the details of the death of a Dublin doctor, one Christmas, with a delicate skill, using several documents to tell the tale. The reputable Dr. Crawley, apprentice to the late Dr. Burton, a leading authority on mental disorders, is found dead, having poisoned himself. The jury attributes the death to suicide while insane. However, the inquest physician, Dr. O'Neill, has retained a vital piece of evidence from his statement, one which he intends to keep secret until his decease. While it throws no doubt on Crawley's ill state of mind, it suggests that his latter-day work on "opisthophobia"—"fear of the indefinable something behind"—has a darker origin.

The story "cannot be recommended to the neurasthenic, to whom the 'terror' is only too constant a reality," wrote the reviewer for the *Irish Times*. "Indeed, the stories remind us of Poe—not imitatively, since they are original in imaginative sense and working out, but in the ease and simplicity with which the writer handles figments of the brain as actual incidents" (28 January 1924).

Here, Cearnach showed himself an empathetic student of contemporary psychology and, in the essay "The Nervous Child", a study of the childhood fears of Dickens and others, he decried the "phobias that obsess [one]". In the child especially, these fears are made worse by scolding and censure and can lead to terrible outcomes. "From the psychological point of view," he continued, "there is nothing more harmful than the production of artificial complexes to check impulses which are already suffering from the effects of repression due to environment."

In the volume of Diarmuid Breathnach and Máire Ní Mhurchú's series of Irish language biographies, *Beathaisnéis* (1986), it is stated that "The Fiend That Walks Behind" was originally published in 1921, but there is no reference as to where (or even if) the other stories in *The Fatal Move* were published elsewhere. In the *Irish Times* notice of his passing, his literary accomplishments are noted, including a book with the erroneous title *The Fiend That Walks Behind* taking the place of *The Fatal Move*—perhaps in the intervening years, literary taste had caught up. "The Fiend That Walks Behind" was reprinted in *The Green Book 15* (Spring 2020).

The author's reading around psychology comes up again in "The Homing Bone", in which a Scottish anatomist plunders an ancient bone while on a trip to Dublin and is haunted by a succession of uncanny dreams until the bone returns to its rightful resting place. One might be reminded of M. R. James's "A Warning to the Curious", in which the young Paxton uncovers a lost crown of East Anglia and is mercilessly haunted to return it. That story was first published in the August 1925 issue of *The London Mercury*, the year after Cearnach's small volume, so it is likely they were influenced by similar reading by the two authors.

Certainly, Cearnach read with interest about sleep and dreams and seemed more swayed by the physiological nature of dreaming than the psychoanalytical. In the essay "Dream Stuff", he relates how recent experiments show the effect of the surrounding environment on the nature of dreams: when a nurse shines a light across the closed eyes of sleeping patients, one man dreams of fire, another (a sailor) dreams of lightning at sea. "The dream seems to work backward from what was really a starting-point, so as to write an introduction to it." In a corresponding essay, "Sleeplessness", he suggests that it is possible to induce dreams artificially: "by uncovering the feet of a sleeper we make him dream that he is walking on water."

Gillespie, the anatomist, boasts of never having dreamed dreams before now, but, after encountering the Homing Bone, "in that dark room, in the small hours of the morning there were stirrings of the hereditary fears—the fear of the dark and the fear of the dead." These are the same instinctive fears that Cearnach wrote of in "The Nervous Child", natural to each from birth and better soothed than repressed. These are ancient impulses easily stirred by worry, loneliness, and the sense of being far from home: all of which Gillespie experiences at the British Medical Association conference. Like the sailor, who dreams of lightning at sea, an anatomist might fill in his dreamscape with the fittings of his trade: not only skeletons, but a fluorescent screen on which "powerful Röntgen Rays" detailed a skiagraph.

In his final experience with the bone, a paralysed Gillespie hears somebody enter his room and open the portmanteau in which he believes the bone is hidden. He is certain that he is not asleep. However, his experience here is somewhat similar to the one Bergson outlines and that Cearnach quotes: the barking dog next-door is transmogrified into the baying crowd of his dream. Gillespie, hearing something in his "quiet lodgings", has created a narrative for himself to rationalise his hereditary fears. In this way, he is no different to his ancestors with their second-sight or the Chinese physicians (rather than the Viennese students of "The Fiend That Walks Behind") that interpret dreams.

Similarly, Gillespie's colleague tries to account for the anatomist's experience through a diagnosis, but nothing fully comes together. A contemporary review criticised a story that "gives us a mystery but attempts no solution", but current sensibilities might see such ambiguity as the point. This is reflected in Gillespie's uncertainty over the genesis of the femur: did it belong to an Irishman or a Viking? Modern expertise can tell us only so much. There are some things too ancient to know for sure and, yet, there are things we can be certain are always true: fear, darkness, death.

Perhaps this is a bleak standpoint to put on an Anglican clergyman. However, these things do join us in humanity: the

Celt and the Dane; the Scot and the Irishman; the rationalist and the dreamer. Cearnach locates "The Homing Bone" in St. Werburgh's, a twelfth century Church of Ireland chapel, built on the pre-Anglican parish of St. Martin of Tours. In its churchyard, the commander-in-chief of the United Irishmen, Edward Fitzgerald, was buried alongside Henry Sirr, the soldier who arrested him and delivered him to his execution. It is a place with its own complexities in a complex city. Whether the Homing Bone wants to return to the sanctified ground of the churchyard or to some older burial place is perhaps unimportant.

Orientalism and its associated stereotypes creep up again in "Professor Danvers' Disappearance", when a private detective—but by no means an occult detective—retells the case of the eponymous professor, a locked-room mystery where only the scholar's clothes remain after a visit from an unknown man in a turban. A review in *Studies: An Irish Quarterly Review*, March 1924, considered it "the most original and striking story told in the book", which seems an unusual opinion as the piece is, in many ways, the most conventional and rational in the collection.

The review is correct in that the story could use "a little more elaboration", as "the author is in too great a hurry to get his story through". The mystery and its solution are expounded very quickly, when the plot, with its academic setting and a sceptic's sardonic references to *The Occult Review*, *Light*, and the *Society for Psychical Research*, could easily have been paced to the short novel-length in the style of John Dickson Carr, if not, as the review suggests "a 'shocker' such as we have often been thrilled with by Poe or W. W. Jacobs (when in that vein)". The *Irish Times* was also satisfied: "the solution is Chestertonian in its completeness and unexpectedness" (1 January 1924).

There is little to suggest that Cearnach had the interest or stamina for longer work, outside of translation. Danvers may even be a reference to Sir Danvers Carew, a minor character in *Strange Case of Dr. Jekyll and Mr. Hyde*, which Cearnach might already have been working on.

The same *Irish Quarterly* reviewer describes the final story in the collection as "the weakest story that the author tells", which, with hindsight, seems as misguided as their evaluation of "Professor Danvers' Disappearance".

"The Rejuvenation of Smithovitch" is a delightfully comic dystopia, in which England has been taken over by Bolshevik Russia and the English language wiped out much to the amusement of our *Gaeilgeoir* narrator. The last living English speaker John Smith, or Ivan Smithovitch as he is known, officially seeks a dangerous medical procedure to prolong his life and, thus, save the language.

The *Irish Quarterly* thought "the humour is feeble and forced", but seems to miss the irony so frequent in Cearnach's writing. Significant to the author, and perhaps lost on an English-language publication (even an Irish one), is the fact that the story is published in English, while the narrator assures us that he doesn't know the language and that all his exchanges with Smith are conducted in "the worst bad Gaelic ever spoken". In the world of the story, the death of English can only be shared in Irish; but, if the story itself was in Irish, it would be unintelligible to the vast majority of O'Connell's readers.

In the early twenties, a Bolshevik takeover of England seemed very unlikely. However, Sir Edward Carson, the figurehead of Unionism in the North, made public statements to the effect that Sinn Féin represented a Bolshevist conspiracy in Ireland. He founded the Ulster Unionist Labour Association as a means of keeping "Bolsheviks and Republicans" out of local labour movements. In the sectarian violence that dominated Northern Ireland in its early years, the UULA created an "unofficial special constabulary" comprised of union members to protect Protestant areas, eventually receiving government endorsement and funding as the B Specials.

The *Irish Times* of 27 February 1918 saw Bolshevist tendencies in Sinn Féin's appeals to the "greed and jealousy of the poorer classes". While, in November 1920, a visiting American, George L. Fox, told the *Liverpool Post* that "the independence of Ireland was a Bolshevik scheme for the robbery of the loyal citizens of the United Kingdom".

Perhaps the term was not well-understood, as, after he threatened to unleash the Ulster Volunteer Force on 12 July 1919, the *Daily Mail* described Carson himself as "a Bolshevist who intends to rouse passion at a moment when freedom-loving Britons are desirous of burying an old feud to establish a free national Government in Ireland".

In a commons debate of April 1921, the right honourable Sir F. Hall stated it was proven that there were direct connections between Sinn Féin and Russian Bolshevists, to which Lieutenant-Commander Kenworthy, M.P. for Kingston-upon-Hull Central, replied: "If the connection is so close between Sinn Féiners and the Germans, how can it also be so close between Sinn Féiners and Bolsheviks? Cannot you make up your minds which to choose?"

O'Connell was no particular fan of Bolshevism, but nor did he see it as a credible threat to his home. Ireland was no fit for it.

"Under the Bolshevist regime in Russia, the office of Minister of Education was given to the village postman. Russians have little or no sense of humour. It is a thousand pities that there was no Irishman on the local Soviet committee to point out, even at the risk of execution, that it would be impossible to find among the proletariat a person more eminently qualified for the position seeing that the postman was undoubtedly a 'man of letters'!"

That "feeble and forced" humour is decidedly an Irish humour. Indeed, it is the Dublin-based *Freeman's Journal* that recognises "Smithovitch" as the only story in the collection "in his usual style" and O'Connell's satire is intended for an Irish audience (10 April 1924). In "Patriotism and Language", he noted that a German can say "Germany is my native land and I speak German", but that the Irishman must say "Ireland is my native land and I speak English; I am proud of my native land but I have no native tongue. I speak a kind of Esperanto—a language that had its origin in a neighbouring island, but it is the common property of nearly 200 millions of varying colours and countries."

This is the psychic gap that the non-Irish reader may struggle to bridge, that there is a language, and a culture and worldview with it, from which the Irish reader has been cut off. Were the story written in Irish, as the characters experience it, it would be as unintelligible to as many Irish readers as to readers elsewhere.

The story is not a broadside against the British then—or not solely. O'Connell acknowledges that the Sassenachs "once proscribed the Irish language in this country", but, ultimately, he holds the Irish themselves responsible for the fate of their language, for not valuing it, for turning it into a political plaything and not uniting around it, regardless of one's persuasion. "The purely English-speaking Irishman has no true historical perspective. For him Irish history begins with the year '98, or the Battle of the Boyne, or the landing of Strongbow. For such short-sightedness the study of the Irish language is an excellent corrective. It enables one to realise that Irish history is not confined to the last 700 years."

Not every Irish reader recognised Cearnach's intention, as shown by the *Irish Quarterly* review, and, certainly, on a non-Irish reader, it would be lost entirely; "The Rejuvenation of Smithovitch" may well seem an absurdity. But he meant it to be read by those in Ireland—both Nationalist and Unionist—as a warning. If you lose your language, you lose your history and that leaves only a future on the margins. When John Smith is the last living English-speaker, does not his untranslatable speech sound like the man-monkey gibberish of the Irishman in the *Punch* cartoons?

"Stories of this kind are, not uncommonly, repellent," P. I. O'Leary, of *The Advocate*, wrote in summation of the book. "The grisly and the horrifying are often overdone and made extravagant and exaggerated. In his tales of the terrible, however, Conall Cearnach has succeeded in investing the weird and the improbable with a robe of likelihood and actuality that is a tribute to his artistic gifts. His characters are human and lifelike." O'Leary's opinion may not chime with a reading of "The Rejuvenation of Smithovitch", but perhaps modern readers will agree that there is "art in this book".

Even his harsh critic in the *Irish Quarterly* admitted that "Conall Cearnach has, one should say, a future before him as a writer of short stories." However, little or no further fiction seems to have been published.

Despite its merits, Cearnach's work does not seem to feature in any of the classic ghost story anthologies of the twentieth century, where it might have easily sat comfortably alongside the works of Poe, Le Fanu, M. R. James, and others. A great many reputations of Victorian and Edwardian writers have been ushered through the decades by such popular anthologies, as subsequent editors often mined the same canonical material, perpetuating tales of terror until some curious future scholar is moved to investigate an otherwise dimly-remembered name. Cearnach's fiction did not escape literary oblivion until "The Homing Bone" was reprinted in the *Poolbeg Book of Irish Ghost Stories* (1990) edited by David Marcus—it was subsequently perpetuated by the editor of *Classic Tales of the Supernatural* (2001) and *Great Ghost Stories:*

34 Classic Tale of the Supernatural (2002). As an Irishman and hobbyist fiction writer, publishing during a period of political upheaval no less, Cearnach faced a struggle to be recognised and remembered—a trend we hope to remedy with this new edition of his work.

III.

Half of the stories in *The Fatal Move* take place in Dublin. It was a city that O'Connell knew well from his school and college days, as well as he knew Connemarra and Belfast, and as different from both of them. He left Queen's University in 1925, as Helen had grown seriously ill and the only treatment was available in the capital of what was by-then the Irish Free State. She died the same year.

Shortly after, he married Marcella Graham, a Catholic. It is disputed whether or not O'Connell converted to Catholicism, with the *Derry Journal* suggesting he was baptised on 24 November 1924 in the Holy Cross Church, in the Ardoyne area of Belfast, which predates the death of his first wife. Another late account places him on the Council of the Central Catholic Library.

He was an active part of artistic and political circles in Dublin. This began as early as January 1922, when he attended the ill-fated Irish Race Congress in Paris alongside the likes of Éamonn de Valera, Eoin Mac Neill, Douglas Hyde, W. B. and Jack B. Yeats, and the Countess Markievicz.

The congress, proposed by the Irish Republican Association of South Africa, was devised initially to recognise the third anniversary of the declaration of the Irish Republic. However, this was quickly supplanted by a cultural agenda to exhibit the unity, diversity, and achievements of the Irish at home and abroad, regardless of their political beliefs—a programme much to O'Connell's liking. Delegates came from all over the world, wherever Irish people had made their home. This included parties from Argentina, Brazil, Mexico, and Java. Lecpoldo O'Donnell y Lara, the Duke of Tetuan, a Spanish Grandee and distant heir to the O'Donnells of Tyrconnell, was made honorary president of the event.

However, the supposedly apolitical event hit a speed bump when the Irish government approved the Anglo-Irish Treaty—the agreement that ended the Irish War of Independence—a fortnight before the congress opened in France. The passing vote was narrow and the pro- and anti-treaty parties found themselves attending a celebration of Irish unity, when Ireland was anything but. The Civil War that started soon after would continue until May 1923, the period in which *The Fatal Move* went to publication.

The years that followed saw efforts to establish a cultural identity for the Irish State. This included the establishment of a national radio service. On 1 January 1926, a state service began broadcasting in Dublin, under the call signal 2RN, with Seamus Clandillon as director. Complaints were received immediately that the station offered both insufficient content in Irish and too much content in Irish. The truth was that the station was poorly funded and starved for content. O'Connell was approached to provide talks, in both Irish and English, and he obliged with the same wide range and playfulness that characterised his essays. He spoke on such subjects as grammar, the tradition of the Wren Boys, and Connaughtmen—the station director himself was from Gort, Co. Galway.

In 1927, O'Connell was appointed Assistant Director of Broadcasting at the station. Maurice Gorham recounts that "Clandillon had got his long-promised Assistant Director and an exceptionally good one". His responsibilities involved communicating with foreign-language radio stations and, on 1 January 1929, he shared New Year's greetings on air in ten different languages. He received appreciative letters from listeners in Holyhead, who were able to pick up the Dublin station, when he spoke to them in Welsh. "His linguistic abilities are such," the *Irish Times* said on his appointment, "that it would be difficult to find a radio station in the world in which he would not make a competent announcer—even in China" (25 February 1928).

As with his appointment in Belfast, his engagement at 2RN was not without controversy. The Catholic Church expressed its shock and disappointment that an Anglican clergyman should be given a position of such import at the national broadcaster of a newly independent Catholic nation. This throws up further questions about the understanding that O'Connell converted to Catholicism, a question that caused great concern on his sudden, tragic death and remains unanswered.

He spent 19 October 1929 as on-air announcer, filling in for the absent Seamus Hughes. Later that evening, at 8.30 PM, O'Connell and Marcella left their home at 30 Upper Mount Street to go to dinner with Éamon de Valera, then leader of the opposition, and his wife, Sinéad. At the junction of Pembroke Road and Lansdown Road, O'Connell was hit by a bus, his skull, jaw, and two ribs fractured. He died instantly.

Supposedly, the Last Rites were performed by a Catholic priest from a church on Haddington Road, although the only church on Haddington Road is St. Mary's, an Anglican church. It was two days before O'Connell's fifty-third birthday and, only a fortnight earlier, the first production of *Devil Kidneys*, a "short story by Conall Cearnach, the Assistant Director of the Dublin Broadcasting Station", adapted for the stage by John McCann, had taken place at the Father Mathew Hall (*Irish Times*, 2 October 1929).

The bus driver was charged with O'Connell's death and the coroner couldn't help but remark on the passing: "Through the death of Dr. O'Connell the country had lost a great man. His life was devoted to one great ideal, the nationalisation of the language. He stood for all that was good, and for the preservation of national traditions and practices."

O'Connell's body was returned to the west of Ireland to be buried where he had been born. Reports conflict over what happened next, but, in every instance, the scenes are antithetical to the life that O'Connell lived.

According to the *Irish Times*, "the manner of his death and burial had echoes of his eccentricity. When his remains were brought by train to Clifden, both Catholics and Protestants crowded into the station to claim them. Two graves had been prepared: O'Connell being a High Church Protestant and attending Mass occasionally with his new Catholic wife, was mistakenly thought to have converted to Catholicism" (27 August 1993).

In another report, a dispute arose over whether he should have a Protestant or Catholic funeral. When no one would transport the coffin to the Anglican church, it fell to O'Connell's eldest son, Dr. Maurice O'Connell, to drive the coach. The family stayed with the body, in the church, overnight to prevent it from being stolen and buried elsewhere.

In yet another account, a fray broke out at Clifden train station between Archdeacon William Morgan O'Connell, Frederick's father, and Monsignor McAlpine, priest of the local Catholic parish. The Archdeacon, who was described as "the late" in a different *Irish Times* account, but as Rural Dean of Tuam from 1944 in *Crockford's Clerical Directory*, won custody of his son's body, but, as he walked away, the priest called behind him: "You may have his body, but we have his soul." The truth of that statement remains to be seen.

If any of these accounts are wholly accurate, or even partially accurate, it shows little had changed in Ireland between the start and end of the 1920s. As in "The Fatal

Move", the matter of life and death was, for some, about capturing pieces.

F. W. O'Connell is buried at Ballinakill, Moynard, Co. Galway—a homing bone returning to rest. On Monday, 21 October, 2RN broadcast a minute of silence at 1.30 PM, the time when "Conall Cearnach" was next scheduled to speak on air.

The *Irish Times* reported his death with regret: "In Irish literary circles, in particular, there was no better known or popular writer than Conall Cearnach." He was acknowledged as a singular talent, taken too soon: "One always felt that his gifts and rare knowledge ought to have yielded some considerable work."

In the end, O'Connell produced no single "considerable work". However, with this new edition of *The Fatal Move*, we hope to show F. W. O'Connell—"Conall Cearnach"—for who he was: a man of many ideas, reaching in many directions, and never settling on one thing. His interests were as wide as his knowledge was deep and his view of human history was long.

Might *The Fatal Move* constitute a glimpse of the considerable work O'Connell could have produced? It seems unlikely. *The Fatal Move* may well best be compared to *White Spirits and Black* (1895) by Ralph Adams Cram or *November Night Tales* (1928) by Henry C. Mercer, curious one-off volumes of outré literature never to be repeated. They represent weird tangents in careers spent elsewhere; not their most celebrated achievements; curious, but no less notable addenda. Almost one hundred years after it was published, *The Fatal Move* is presented again with a selection of Cearnach's essays, reintroducing the collection into a time almost as tumultuous, divided, and uncertain; in need of a gentler view of humanity. Maybe these stories will make as much sense of the world now as they did then.

Perhaps "Conall Cearnach" must stand as F. W. O'Connell's "considerable work"—as little as we know of him—a man of great modesty, a master of strange tongues.

Reggie Chamberlain-King
Whitehead, Northern Ireland
January 2021

The Fatal Move

The Fatal Move

Men are apt to find a common vice closer bond of union than a common virtue; that is why boon companions are so inseparable. It was a common vice which cemented the friendship of Pierre Régnaud and François Dubert: for each of them was a veritable chess-fiend. They devoted all their spare moments, as well as many moments which they could ill afford to spare, to the ancient game. They carried about in their pockets miniature sets, in which the pieces were held in position by a special device, so that the whole thing could be folded up and put away until there was an opportunity of resuming the game. On top of the omnibus one might see Régnaud with his chess-board on his knee, deep in the solution of a problem; while at the self-same moment Dubert would be found speeding to his office by the Métro, as the Parisians call their Underground Railway, engaged in a similar solution. Every evening they met either at the Café de la Régence or at the Café de l'Univers; where they would sit at a circular table with a chess-board between them, and a tall glass of *café noir* at their elbows.

Régnaud was by profession an electrical engineer; Dubert was in the silk trade; and both were unmarried. There had been a time when they had seriously contemplated matrimony. That was when Jeannette, the only daughter of old Armand Muset, the *advocat*, returned from finishing her education at the convent school. For a month or two they were unremitting in their attentions to Jeannette; but old Muset had laid his plans beforehand, and he bestowed the hand of the fair Jeannette upon the wealthy Alphonse Feuillard, who was fifteen years her senior. It was obviously a *mariage de convenance*, like most French middle-class marriages. Muset was a miser, and Feuillard was quite prepared to waive the question of a *dot*; the affair was simple.

Any jealousy that threatened to break the friendship of Régnaud and Dubert vanished into thin air. They renounced all idea of marrying, and directed their thoughts towards chess tournaments instead. For ten years they kept talking of nothing but gambits and defences, knights and castles, and mate in so many moves; and the probabilities are that they would have continued chess-playing until death did them part, but the Great War arrived and made many strange moves on the chess-board of Europe. The Armistice found the inseparables still sound in wind and limb, though bearing minor scars; but a German shell had removed one piece clean off the board, to wit, Feuillard; and when Régnaud and Dubert returned to Paris they found the fair Jeannette, a war-widow at twenty-seven, more adorable than ever.

They called to condole with her as a matter of formal politeness; for it was common knowledge that Feuillard's taking-off came as a relief to his relict; the Feuillard *ménage* had not proved a happy one. The calls became more frequent as the months went by, and the inseparable friends took to calling on the pretty widow separately. This was the first rift within the lute of their friendship. They met no more at the Café de la Régence or at that of the Univers. They even ceased to speak when they met in the street. They were rivals. The flame of jealousy burned deeply in the soul of Régnaud. He arrived at the door of Madame Feuillard's residence in the Avenue Kléber, one afternoon, in time to see Dubert taking his departure. Dubert seemed in excellent humour, and he bowed stiffly to his rival. Régnaud glowered at him and muttered under his breath: "Nevertheless I shall win the game; before long I shall checkmate him."

Now, to give the widow her due, she was a stickler for the proprieties; and she gave both her suitors clearly to understand that any attempts at paying court to her until the period of official mourning was at an end would be displeasing to her. Either was welcome as a caller *en bon ami*, be it understood: but that was all. Afterwards, who knows? Meantime she treated both alike as very good old friends. Régnaud had just as much reason for being in a good humour as had Dubert, if the insanity of jealousy would permit it. And it was a very real insanity; for there was a streak of lunacy in the Régnaud family, and Pierre's maternal uncle had ended his days in the Maison de Santé, at Charenton—the Bedlam of France. With all the cunning of a lunatic, Pierre changed his tactics. He blew into Dubert's office in the Rue St. Honoré, one afternoon, and insisted on carrying him off to the Café de la Régence. There, over a glass of *café noir*, he apologised for his bearish behaviour.

"François, *mon ami*," he declared, "it is unthinkable that such close friends as we two should quarrel, even over the adorable Jeannette. The truth is that since I have neglected the chess-board my temper has not been quite so equable. If we are rivals for the hand of Madame Feuillard—what of it? Let us forget our enmity in the mental distractions provided by the noble game of chess. I challenge you once more—no, not here in the Café de la Régence—you must come down to my villa at Argenteuil. Come to dinner on Thursday. Will that suit your convenience? Good; it is an affair concluded. After dinner we shall play out into the small hours, *comme autrefois*. Until Thursday, then! *Au revoir!*" They shook hands and parted.

On Thursday evening, Dubert left Paris by the 6.30 train from the Gare St. Lazare, and punctually at seven o'clock he was admitted to Régnaud villa by old deaf Jules, Régnaud's factotum. They sat down to dinner, and all through the meal Régnaud chattered incessantly. He drank no wine, yet his eyes seemed preternaturally bright, and his face was flushed. Then came the inevitable cups of *café noir*, and when they had been despatched Régnaud produced cigars. But he was consumed with impatience.

"Come!" he cried, "let us finish our cigars over an opening game; the first of a series."

He led the way to a room at the rere, overlooking some outhouses, from one of which proceeded the hum of a dynamo; for Régnaud supplied his own electric light, and the house was full of all sorts of labour-saving devices worked by the current from his private plant. He threw open the door of the room, and motioned Dubert to enter.

"*Voilà, mon ami*," he cried. "I am not fishing for compliments, but I think you will admit that as a chess-room this apartment is unique."

The walls of the room were covered with glass cases containing a valuable collection of chess boards and chessmen from all parts of the world. There were beautifully inlaid boards from Persia and China and India. A history of the game might almost be compiled from a close study of the objects in the various cases. One curio which Régnaud pointed out with pride was an ancient Irish chessman in bronze. The only furniture in the room consisted of a large chess-table, with squares of polished white and black inlaid. At opposite sides of the chess-table stood two large arm-chairs of unusual shape. They appeared to be made of some heavy wood, such as oak, and the backs of the chairs were high enough to reach above the head of the average sitter. They sat down in the chairs at the table, on which the chessmen were already arranged in readiness for a game. Dubert remarked that such valuable boards would prove a temptation to burglars.

"My friend," replied Régnaud, "the most valuable board in the room is the table at which we are sitting; but I defy *Messieurs les voleurs* to steal it. Like the chairs on which we sit, the table is made from solid steel, and is bolted to the floor. If you will have the goodness to lift one of the pieces, you will observe that they, too, are heavy, being made of metal also. It was the ancient Irish chessman that gave me the idea. Do you find your chair comfortable?"

Dubert, who was leaning back lazily, puffing at his cigar, with his hands resting along the arms of his chair, declared that it was perfect.

"Nevertheless, I can easily convert it into a chair which gives to the figure a support similar to that given to infants by their nursery-chairs. I but press this button with my foot, and *voilà*!" As he spoke, two semi-circular bands of steel flew out from the inside of the chair-arms and locked themselves around the waist of Dubert; and simultaneously a hasp of steel swung up from underneath the left chair-arm and neatly pinned Dubert's left wrist.

Dubert spluttered in astonishment, and dropped his cigar.

"*Mon Dieu!*" he exclaimed. "What is the meaning of this?"

"It is quite simple, *mon ami*. You see the circlet of steel around your waist supports your figure; the hasp on the left confines your left hand, but you have your right hand free to play chess. What more do you want?

"Now, if you will attend carefully, for a few moments, I shall explain fully the advantages of the chairs and of the table and pieces."

Dubert stared in bewildered fashion at his host, and read in his eyes something which caused him to shriek with terror. "Help! Help!" he screamed. "You devil! Would you murder me in cold blood? Let me go! Let me go!"

Régnaud shrugged his shoulders deprecatingly; then he held up his hand for silence.

"You excite yourself unduly, *mon ami*," he said. "Why waste your voice in shouting when the room is sound-proof, and in any case Jules is stone deaf? Besides, I have no intention of 'murdering' you, as you so vulgarly express it. If you will only have patience I shall explain. I invited you here to play a game of chess. *Eh, bien*! we are going to play it; and I can assure you that it is the most unique game of chess that has ever been played.

"In the first place the pedestal of this table conceals a cable conveying an electric current to one square of each side of the board; a similar cable is attached to the steel chairs. Now it is obvious, even to those who are not experts in electrical engineering, that if contact should be established in such a way that the current flowing to the table should pass to either chair through the body of its occupant, the result is at once imaginable."

Here he was interrupted by the renewed outcries of the terrified Dubert.

"I had no idea, *mon ami*, that you were such a coward," said Régnaud. "Will you not have patience to hear the whole explanation? I am taking exactly the same risks as yourself. *Voyons*! Be reasonable."

Dubert could only gibber feebly, for he was prostrated with terror, and the drops of perspiration stood out upon his brow, while his countenance turned a sickly green.

"As I was saying," resumed Régnaud, "I am not asking you to take any risk which I am not prepared to take myself. To proceed. The problem was to effect this contact and complete the circuit in an ingenious and original manner. This is where the ancient Irish chessman gave me an inspiration. All my chessmen are made of copper, which, as you doubtless are aware, is an excellent conductor of electricity. Further, the under surfaces of all of them are covered with a special insulating material invented by myself; all, that is, except one piece on each side. I do not myself know which are the two pieces which are not so protected, for it was Jules who carried out the insulation, and I merely instructed him to leave one white piece and one black piece uninsulated. You see, then, that we run exactly the same risk, we two. The only advantage I have over you, if it is an advantage, is that I know at the present moment under which squares the electric cables are situated; I tested the wiring before dinner. However, in order to be on an exact equality with you in every respect, I shall now touch this button which gives to the arrangement beneath the surface of the table a spin like that of a roulette wheel. By the time the mechanism has once more come to rest—a fact which will be heralded by a distinct click—I shall not know any more than you which of the squares are electrified. There it is. Did you hear the click? Now we shall go on with the game. And, mark you, the rules of the game must be strictly adhered to, just as at the Café de la Régence. During the course of the game it is possible that either you or I shall innocently move an uninsulated piece on to one of the electrified squares; in which case a current of four thousand volts will be discharged through the body of one of us; and that will be, in the most literal sense of the word, checkmate—*échec et mat*—the latter word, as you know, is the Persian for 'dead'. One other point of interest—in fact the real starting-point and *raison d'etre* of this unique contest—the winner, or in other words, the survivor, is free to pay his addresses to Madame Feuillard, unhampered by arrival."

The mention of Madame Feuillard's name seemed to wake up Dubert from a state of coma. "And if I refuse to play?" he asked; "you may hold me prisoner in this accursed chair, but you cannot force me to play, you demon!"

"In that case, *mon ami*," replied the imperturbable Régnaud, "I shall very reluctantly be forced to take other measures. If I were so disposed I could easily electrocute you as you sit there; and then, carrying your body downstairs to the power-house, I could summon assistance and explain that you had accidentally touched a live wire from the dynamo, thus electrocuting yourself. But we will not dwell on such unpleasant thoughts. Let me rather appeal to your love of the romantic. What would Jeannette think if she learnt that I, Pierre Régnaud, was prepared to risk my life to win her, while you were afraid to risk yours? Again, let me appeal to your love of sport. As a confirmed chess-player, can you imagine a more exciting game than one in which the finish may mean for either player a quick and painless death on the one hand, or on the other, a free field and his heart's desire?

"If I should lose the game, a certain thermos-electric apparatus, which is attached to the wristlet of my chair-arm, will function in such a way that the loss of temperature due to the cooling of my body after death will set in motion a mechanism which will release from these chairs both the corpse and the living survivor. My doctor is aware that I suffer from a certain valvular disease of the heart, and he will not consider an inquest necessary. There will be no need for you to divulge any of our private proceedings; and nobody will dream of arresting you on a charge of being in any way connected with my death. In case you lose—but you need not trouble about subsequent happenings; I shall merely mention that since your chair-arm is not equipped with a thermos-electric apparatus, I should be obliged to bring into play a small switch situated on my side of the table in order to release your remains from your chair. See! I press this button, and *vlan*! I, too, am imprisoned as to my waist and handcuffed to the chair-arm by the left wrist, leaving my right hand to move my pieces.

"Let us waste no more time. Since you really have no choice but to play, let me entreat you to commence. Remember that you must really play your best. Bear in mind that it is always possible that neither of us may in the course of the game place one of the non-insulated pieces on an electrified square. We may play the game to the ordinary finish. If it proves to be a stale-mate, then we shall have to play a second game. What I want to bring home to you is that if either of us is checkmated the loser is bound in honour as a Frenchman, and a gentleman, to retire from the field and renounce Jeannette. You make the first move!"

All the time Régnaud was speaking, he kept his burning eyes fixed upon the eyes of Dubert; and it would almost seem as though he hypnotised him into obedience; for, silently and mechanically, he seized a pawn at random and made the first move. Régnaud chuckled. "Pray accept my felicitations, *mon ami*," he observed. "You have invented a new gambit. In future let it be known in the annals of chess as the Dubert gambit. All the same, I have a distinct presentiment that I shall win the game. The excitement due to the bizarre novelty of this game goes to my head like champagne; but I shall refrain from speaking."

The game proceeded in silence. By the time that half-a-dozen pieces on each side had been removed the players were intent upon their game. Brows were furrowed with deep thought. So intent were both men that they quite forgot their gamble with death. They became oblivious of their pinioned bodies and fettered left hands. It was as though they sat again at their accustomed table at the Café de la Régence. At the end of half-an-hour it was evident that the Dubert gambit was not destined to lead to victory. Moving up his sole remaining bishop, Régnaud shouted, "Check!" Dubert just managed to save himself by moving his king one square. Once more came the cry of "Check!" The game was almost ended. Régnaud's eyes glittered with a maniacal light as he lifted a knight and made the final move.

"Check!" he screamed, triumphantly. "Check and mate!

Échec et mat!" At the last word he placed the piece on its proper square, and as he did so a convulsive shudder shook his frame. Every muscle in his body appeared to stiffen for a second, and then his form became limp and lifeless. His right hand fell to his side, sweeping his few remaining pieces from the table. He was dead. Dubert stared for one moment at the corpse facing him, and then he fainted away.

In the morning Jules found him still seated in the chair, although the mechanism had released the confining circlet and fetter. He was raving about gambits and electric squares. The shock and reaction affected him so much that for a month the doctors despaired of his reason. But he recovered; and by that time Régnaud was long lying in Père la Chaise. He had been buried without an inquest, as he foretold. It was surmised that he had died suddenly of heart disease, and that the shock of his sudden death had overcome Dubert to the extent of temporarily depriving him of his normal faculties. It was his last game of chess. To this day he cannot hear the mention of the word, much less the sight of a chess-board. So his wife told me, for I had the tale from the lips of Madame Jeannette Dubert herself.

The Vengeance of the Dead

Chandranath Chatterjee was a Heathen Hindoo. In appearance there was nothing to distinguish him from the typical Indian student of our Universities; he wore a turban and the inevitable gold-rimmed spectacles; his nose fell short of the aquiline by being blunt-tipped and thick about the nostrils; his form was slender, lithe and sinuous, and his footfall was silent. He had come to Trinity ostensibly to study Law; and his progress in the Law School was slow, and he had "funked" several examinations. Yet in arts he had somehow managed to obtain a pass degree, and his name appeared over the door of his chambers in the usual letters of white upon a black ground: CH. CHATTERJEE, M.A.

His pet abomination was a compatriot named Mustapha Ali, a medical student who had rooms at the corner of our square; and the hatred was returned with compound interest. I never could quite fathom the reason for this mutual antipathy. At first sight one might be inclined to attribute it to religious animosities, for Ali was a pious Mohammedan; but Chatterjee was by no means an orthodox Hindoo—his religion being a vague Theism of the kind inculcated by the Arya Samaj, seasoned with a dash of the gospel according to Mrs. Besant and modern spiritualism. I think, too, that it was largely out of sheer devilment that Ali pretended that his righteous soul was vexed by the bronze image of Ganesha which stood on Chatterjee's mantelpiece.

Be that as it may, the fact remains that the sight of Ali's red fez had the effect on Chatterjee which the proverbial red rag has on a bull. Sometimes the men would not speak for days at a stretch, but the intervals of silence were occupied by weird forms of practical joking. For example, when Ali awoke one morning he found that the B.A. on his door-plate had been altered in the night to BADZAT (Anglice, "Blackguard"); whereupon he promptly revenged himself by changing Chatterjee's M. A. to MARHUM—which is the Molsem way of expressing "the late lamented".

I came to know Chatterjee fairly intimately, owing to the circumstance that his chambers faced mine on the same landing; and also, because, as an Indian Civil Service student, I was working hard at Oriental languages, and frequently discussed points of Hindustani and Sanscrit grammar with him. One evening I sat in his room reading aloud to him from the *Hitopadesa*, when suddenly as though tired of listening to my halting utterance, he began to recite the next lines from memory. It was a revelation to me to hear how grand the ancient language sounded as sonorous Sanscrit syllables came rolling forth from native organs. Then he proceeded to translate it into English, which he pronounced with the pure vowels and clear-cut t's and d's of Hindustani.

"You understand thatt—yess? 'Of all things knowledge is thee best, they say; itt cannot be bought, itt cannot be stolen, itt is imperishable always.' Yess; thatt is veree grand sentiment. See, I have written itt up there over Sri Ganesha's image on the mantelpiece; which image thatt ruffeean, Mustafa Ali, tried to steal thee other day. He said he would break itt in pieces, as Mohammed broke the idol Lat; but I think itt exceedinglee probable he prefer to pawn itt and make pieces of money of itt—yess!"

In order to wean him from the subject of Mustafa's evil ways, I suddenly turned the conversation into another channel.

"By the way, Chatterjee," I said, "is it a fact that you Indians possess more knowledge of the occult than we Westerns, and have you a special gift for that sort of thing?"

"Oa no," he replied. "Oa no, oanlee we are accustomed to manifestations of thee occult for ages; while you have comparativelee lately made acquaintance of occult under names of hypnotism and mesmerism and spiritualism."

"Hypnotism is all right," I said; "there is nothing very occult about it. As for spiritualism, I must confess that I am a rank sceptic in the matter. In India you have lots of Yogis and Fakirs, but they appear to be genuine, so far as one can gather, and deadly in earnest. Over here, if there are any real mediums—which I doubt—they are discredited by the swarm of Sludges who, in spite of frequent exposures, batten on the credulity of elderly maiden ladies and retired lieutenant-colonels."

"Oa yess," he said. "You have, I daresay, manee impostors; but thatt is because you have not thee patience of thee East. You will not wait long enough to develop necessaree stage of Yogi. You rush still undeveloped mediums—and then complain thatt they are frauds—yess!"

"But," I persisted; "can you tell me of one single genuine medium of your acquaintance? Or have you developed mediumistic powers yourself?"

"I know a veree good medium," he replied; "thatt is to say, he is not fully developed—noa; but he has power, and with care itt will increase, yess. I have not thee power myself; but I can do certain things which interest some peepul when I go to spend evenings sometimes. Would you like to see something interesting now—yess?"

He filled a glass—"gilass" he called it—with fresh water, and gave it to me to hold in one hand.

"Now continue to look at that gilass steadilee, always for some time until you see something, and tell me what you see."

I stared intently at the glass as directed—although I felt rather sceptical as to the result of the experiment. At first I could see nothing but *aqua pura*; but after a while my eyes grew tired, and a mist seemed to grow up and swirl round and round in the glass. Gradually the mist began to clear towards the centre: *and finally I saw a distinct picture of a snow-white building under a brilliant sky. There was no mistaking it—the famous Taj Mahall which I had frequently seen in photographs.* I was still gazing at it and attempting to make out details, when it slowly faded away, and I became conscious of holding a glass of clear water once more. I looked up to find Chatterjee beaming at me through his spectacles.

"You have seen something—yess? Whatt is itt you have seen?"

"I saw what looked like the Taj."

"Thatt is exactlee whatt I wished you to see. But why do you say 'looked like'? Did you not see thee veree Taj itself?"

I maintained that the vision I had seen was purely subjective; that it was partly a replica of coloured photographs which I had seen already; and that I believed that by a process of self-hypnotism I could probably call up a similar vision if only I fixed my mind intently on a particular scene.

"Oa, yess; you are veree sceptikul. But I may yet show you things not so easy to explain. If you sitt some evening with me and thee good medium I told you about, you will see some interesting manifestations—veree interesting, yess!"

I promised that when I had my examination over, and could afford to waste an evening, I would willingly give him an opportunity of converting a sceptic.

A few mornings later, I heard sounds of a lively altercation proceeding from Chatterjee's room, and I could catch the excited voice of Ali declaring in voluble Hindustani that if Chatterjee tried any more of his accursed idol-tricks on him, by the holy Kaaba, he (Ali) would throw the image of Ganesha into the Liffey, or break it into a thousand pieces.

Determining to intervene in the interests of peace, I stepped across the landing and knocked at the door. Chatterjee, who opened, hailed my arrival with obvious relief, and asked Ali to repeat his "sillee accusation" in my presence.

Ali's complaint was to the effect that *he had been disturbed in his sleep on two successive nights by a nightmare which took the form of a vision of the elephant-god Ganesha*, who came and squatted on Ali's chest, waving his truck angrily and trying to strangle him with his four arms. This nocturnal visitation he asserted to be the product of Chatterjee's Pagan deviltries, aided and abetted by the Jinn-possessed idol Ganesha, which, together with Chatterjee's wretched neck, he would assuredly break if ever the vision troubled his repose again.

I ventured to suggest a more naturalistic explanation; *viz.*, that the vision was an ordinary nightmare induced by late suppers, and coloured by the fact that Ali had got Ganesha on the brain. Chatterjee seemed to welcome my explanation; but when Ali had left the room, he threw himself into an armchair and gave vent to peal after peal of laughter.

"Oh Ho-Ho!" he roared, "itt is so veree funnee! The sillee felloa—he is not quite so sceptikul as you are. He fears Ganesha and powers of occult—yess!"

"Look here, Chatterjee," I said; "take my advice and find some other subject to try these telepathic or hypnotic tricks on. Don't push it too far with Ali, or you will be sorry one of these days."

I could see, however, that Chatterjee was too delighted with the success of his experiments to think of anything else just then; so I left him with a final word of warning. As though to confirm my explanation of the vision, as due to some disorder of the digestive functions, *Ali was admitted to the fever wing of his own hospital towards the end of that week, suffering from a sharp attack of typhoid*. In his delirium he raved incessantly of Ganesha and Chatterjee;

and the house-surgeon informed me that two nurses were required to hold him down in bed. Just as he was beginning to convalesce, *Ali got a relapse, and he died in a few days from internal haemorrhage.*

The news of Ali's death did not disconcert Chatterjee in the least; in fact, his references to the deceased were so full of pagan hatred and malice and all uncharitableness, that I felt in duty bound to read him a stern lecture on the adage, "*De mortuis nil nisi bonum*," and to warn him that, if he spoke like that in the hearing of Ali's class-mates of the medical school, he would in all probability earn for himself a jolly good kicking. I saw no more of him until the beginning of the Winter Session, when he invited me to his rooms one evening to meet his "veree good medium".

I turned up at his rooms at nine o'clock, and was introduced to the medium—an American rejoicing in the unromantic name of Fitchett. I cannot say that I was favourably impressed by Mr. Fitchett. He was a flabby, pasty-complexioned individual, with damp, fishy hands and shifty eyes. After some desultory conversation on psychic matters in general, he left me to Chatterjee, while he strolled over to the mantelpiece and appeared to become absorbed in the contemplation of our friend Ganesha. In a few minutes Chatterjee produced a small, plain, deal-table; drew the curtains close; placed a fire-screen before the fire, and turned down the burner on his Duplex lamp until only the ghost of a narrow blue ring was showing. Then we took our seats at the table and awaited manifestations. We had sat for, I should think fully twenty minutes, and nothing abnormal had happened. My hands were growing tired of the cramped position they occupied on the table, and I discounted as purely subjective the sensation as of a cold breeze blowing on them. Soon the table began to heave and sway; and short, sharp raps were heard.

"*Ask who thee spirit is!*" suggested Chatterjee.

Fitchett repeated the alphabet slowly three times, pausing after each letter, and the table rapped in the affirmative at the letters A, L, I.

Chatterjee muttered an imprecation under his breath. He was evidently both impressed and uneasy at the same time. All of a sudden the medium's right hand began to work convulsively and to drum rapidly on the table.

"A writing control," whispered Chatterjee, excitedly.

Without rising from his seat, he produced a pencil and writing-tablet from a large table behind him. The medium grasped the pencil and commenced to scribble rapidly. Chatterjeee cried out that something had touched his hair; and the words were scarcely out of his mouth when there was a loud crash at the fire-place. I jumped to my feet and turned up the lamp. Fitchett was lying back in his chair, apparently in a state of great exhaustion. He opened his eyes, sat up and drawled out: "Say! What's the matter?"

Chatterjee had made his way to the fire-place. He stood there grey from terror, pointing with a trembling finger to the hearth. Ganesha had fallen from the mantelpiece, and had broken off a portion of the metal fender. He himself was minus his trunk and one of his arms. Chatterjee picked up the broken idol and restored it to its place; then he rushed to the séance-table and snatched up the paper on which the medium had been scribbling while under "control". Two words were written over and over again.

"See! See!" he cried, and his voice shook with excitement: "Read this!"

"Chatterjee Marhum—Chatterjee Marhum—Chatterjee Marhum."

"Oa yes!" declared Chatterjee. "Itt is undoubtedlee thee spirit of that ruffean Ali. See! he has broken image of Sri Ganesha. We will not s-s-itt anee m-more to-night—noa!"

He was so obviously perturbed that the medium agreed that the "conditions were rayther inharmonious". He thought there should not be a continuation of the séance, as he "sensed an evil hand, right at the start, back of Mr. Chatterjee".

We had some refreshments, and I noticed that the medium stowed away a large quantity of sandwiches and champagne—doubtless in order to counteract the exhaustion subsequent upon the trance. When Fitchett had taken his departure, and an extra "gilass" of champagne had pulled Chatterjee's shaken nerves together, he asked me almost triumphantly whether I could explain the manifestations in my usual "sceptikul" manner.

"I must candidly confess, Chatterjee," said I, "that I am grievously disappointed in you. Here you are, of the East Eastern—you hail from the Land of Mysteries—you come of a race that has had experience of the occult for untold centuries, and you permit yourself to be duped and fooled to the face by a third-rate American 'sharp'. When I came in to-night, I noticed Fitchett poking about Ganesha when your back was turned, and he probably left the image in a position of unstable equilibrium. A long black thread attached to Ganesha's trunk, while the other end was held in Fitchett's teeth, probably did the trick; and it was this thread, as he pulled it taut, that you felt touch your hair."

"Yess! Yess! But thee writing? Chatterjee Marhum—Marhum! Thee medium does not know Arabic!"

"Well," I replied, "you may call it telepathy—or, what is more probable still, he heard you tell about that practical joke of poor Ali's some time or other. I don't profess to explain everything, but, take my word for it, the only spirits that ever come to the call of Fitchett and Company are of the 'Bottled in Bond' variety. Chuck all this silly fooling, and swat up some solid unimaginative Law, and you'll soon be able to go to bed without a light in your room."

"I do not agree with you as regards explanation—noa!" and Chatterjee shook his head solemnly. "Thee manifestations were genuine—Oa yess—otherwise I should be veree angree with Fitchett for breaking Ganesha's image for trick to frighten me. You sceptikul peepul are too readee to believe in fraud. But I agree itt would be better to abandon studee of psychic for thee present—yess!"

For about a week Chatterjee made manful efforts to study Law. He sat in the Library every evening until closing time, because, as he explained to me, he could study there better than in his chambers. Then, one morning, I dropped in to see him and found him perched on a ladder, removing some pictures.

"Yess!? he began in answer to my inquiring look, "I am moving into other rooms. Thee atmosphere of these rooms is stronglee impregnated with Occult. There have been too manee sittings in them."

I promised to look him up in his new quarters, and then passed on down the stairs. Just as I reached the end of the flight, I heard a tremendous clatter, followed by a heavy thud. Remembering the ladder, I tore upstairs three steps at a time, joined by Chatterjee's "skip", who, attracted by the racket, emerged from the second-floor chambers which he had been tidying.

We found Chatterjee lying in a huddled heap on the floor near the fire-place. He had, evidently, overbalanced in trying to remove a large picture which hung over the mantelpiece; and in his fall he had swept all the ornaments with him. I did not like the peculiar angle his head made with his body. We laid him on the hearth-rug, and I sent the "skip" for a senior medical man who lived on the ground floor. He arrived in a few minutes, and made a hurried examination. Then he stood up and looked grave.

"He is stone dead, poor beggar. His neck's broken."

And, as he spoke, I noticed on the hearth-stone the image of Ganesha—now completely armless.

Whenever I tell this story to credulous people, they scout the idea of accident or coincidence, preferring a more weird explanation which lays under contribution the spirit of the late Mustafa Ali. This is, on the face of it, absurd.

The Fiend That Walks Behind

[For the following strange narrative I am indebted to my friend, Mr. George Bartley, of the firm of Messrs. Bartley & Stokes, Solicitors; to whom the documents were entrusted, by their late client, Dr. O'Neill, with a view to their subsequent publication.—C. C.]

Extract from the Irish Times, *December 17, 18—*

"Yesterday afternoon, Dr. Jas. O'Neill, Coroner for South Dublin, held an inquest touching the death of Dr. Robert Crawley, F.R.C.S.I., who was found dead at his residence, 52 Elton Place. Martha Brown, housekeeper to the late Dr. Crawley, deposed to finding deceased sitting in his study armchair; an empty phial labelled "Poison" lay on the floor close to the chair. She immediately summoned Dr. Hughes, in the course of his evidence, stated that when he arrived he found the deceased in the position described by the previous witness. He estimated that Dr. Crawley had then been dead five or six hours. In his opinion death was due to narcotic poisoning. Mrs. Brown, recalled, stated further that deceased had been for some time past eccentric in his habits. He was a bachelor and wealthy. He had retired from practice some months previously. The Coroner, who was visibly affected, said he felt sure they all deplored the sad demise of such a distinguished member of his profession. He had known the late Dr. Crawley for many years. He was one of the foremost authorities on mental disease, and had written some brilliant monographs upon obscure nervous disorders. It was, unfortunately, only too well known that the constant investigation of the various forms of mental disease, and habitual association with the mentally afflicted had before now reacted morbidly on some indefatigable alienists. He felt that the jury would have no hesitation in agreeing on the usual verdict. The jury, without retiring, returned a verdict of suicide during temporary insanity."

STATEMENT BY DR. O'NEILL

The accompanying extract from the *Irish Times* which I cut out and preserved, and have now pinned to this statement, is a brief report of the proceedings at the inquest held upon the remains of the late Dr. Crawley. I wish, now, to state a fact which I deliberately refrained from mentioning at the inquest, *viz.*, that on the morning of the previous day I received by post from Dr. Crawley the strange communication which I herewith enclose. My motives for withholding the information at the time were these: I considered that the verdict returned by the jury was a true one, and formed upon sufficient evidence; and I felt certain that a knowledge of the contents of Crawley's communication would not have influenced them in any way—unless, indeed, it were to confirm them in their conviction as to his insanity. In the second place, I deemed myself justified in suppressing information which might cast a slur upon the memory of the deceased, and, incidentally, upon the good fame of the medical profession in general. My first impulse, indeed, upon reading Crawley's confession, was to destroy it; but respect for his memory, and solicitude for the reputation of our profession, which gave rise, as I have said, to that impulse, were speedily counterbalanced by my instinct as a doctor to preserve every contribution to medical science. Besides, it is now many years since poor Crawley died; and as many more may elapse before these documents see the light, with the lapse of time indignation against a man who is dead and gone becomes more and more impossible. Theoretically, we abhor the memory of a Nero or a Messalina, but practically we are far more incensed towards the cat who has a few moments ago broken our best Sèvres vase. Then, again, the public, which is growing more charitable as it learns more about the vagaries of disordered mentation, will probably regard Crawley's swerve from the strict path of rectitude as merely a premonitory symptom of his particular disorder—like the kleptomania of incipient General Paralysis.

Finally, it will to some extent atone for a slight dereliction of duty on my part which I probably ought to have mentioned at the inquest. I am instructing my solicitors to the effect that the contents of this packet, to wit, the newspaper extract, my statement, and Crawley's confession, shall be published on my decease; the medium of publication to be left to their own discretion and convenience.

(Signed) James O'Neill, M.D.
November 12, 19—

The Confession of Dr. Robert Crawley

I, Robert Crawley, M.D., F.R.C.S.I. and E., until lately practising at 52 Elton Place, Dublin, being to the best of my belief at this present moment of sound mind, do hereby tender an apology to the memory of my colleague, the late Dr. Charles Burton, for having robbed him of posthumous fame; and to the medical profession and the general public for having grossly deceived them by an act of dishonesty which should be abhorrent to all right-minded persons.

In self-justification, perhaps, I may be permitted to plead that it is the one and only offence against the strict code of honour and morality of which I have been guilty during the practice of thirty years. Perhaps, also, I shall not be so harshly condemned when it is known how grievously I have suffered; and how for the last few months of my life, my punishment has been greater than I could bear.

In order to make my narrative perfectly clear, I must begin at the outset of my professional career. Shortly after I became a qualified practitioner, I secured an appointment as medical officer, and, two years later, as medical superintendent of a lunatic asylum. My duties, however, were not congenial to my tastes. I took little interest in the usual forms of insanity; my hobby being the study of the more unusual cases of nervous disease—cases which seldom find their way into even a private asylum; and my pet ambition was to set up a practice as specialist and consultant in obscure neuroses, and to write at my leisure some epoch-making work on the subject.

Accordingly, when Dr. Burton, who had extensive practice of this very kind, advertised for a colleague to assist him in professional work which had become too great a responsibility for one of his advancing years, I applied; and, to my gratification, I was accepted. I soon found, however, to my grievous disappointment, that, although my duties were more congenial than hitherto, I had less time than ever to devote to literary work. As the time went by, Dr. Burton handed over more and more of his patients to my charge, only retaining a few special cases for his own supervision and treatment—which latter consisted in the employment of the method that has now come to be known as psycho-analysis. He had written several books on the subject of mental disease, and still, from time to time, he contributed important articles to the British and foreign medical journals. He confided in me that he had on the stocks a monograph which he intended to form his last contribution to the science of alienation. Under a pledge of secrecy, one evening, he gave me an outline of the subject.

Standing on the hearthrug, after dinner, and adopting the attitude and tone of a lecturer, he said, more to an imaginary audience than to myself—"The various unreasoning, and to the normal mind unreasonable terrors or 'phobias', which account for the eccentric behaviour of certain individuals, have received a scientific classification and nomenclature. Thus, agoraphobia and claustrophobia bear their own explanation and definition as clearly as the terms bronchitis and peritonitis. Now, the phobias which I have mentioned have won general acceptance, and have become part of the vocabulary of medical practitioners, because they are nervous symptoms commonly met with, and may have a considerable duration. There is, however, another 'terror' which, because it is not peculiar to neurotic persons, and because it very rarely lasts long enough to become an obsession, has not hitherto been recognised or studied scientifically. So rarely does it become a lasting symptom that, in the whole course of my thirty-five years' practice as a specialist in nervous diseases, I have only recorded a single case in which this particular phobia was as marked, as constant, and as powerful in affecting the conduct of the patient as the other well-recognised phobias. It is a terror which may suddenly seize upon the sanest individual in certain circumstances, as has been well expressed by the poet when he wrote:—

> *Like one who on a lonely road doth walk*
> *in fear and dread,*
> *And having once looked round, walks on*
> *and turns no more his head,*
> *Because he knows some frightful fiend*
> *doth close behind him tread.*

"The fear, be it noted, is of something indefinable and immaterial; and this fear of the indefinable 'something behind' I have termed 'opisthophobia'.

"In my monograph on the subject, I trace the history of the single and singular case to which I have alluded: a case in which the terror was so persistent as eventually to drive the unfortunate patient to the extremity of taking refuge in self-destruction."

Then reassuming his normal tone of voice, he added: "That's the gist of it, Crawley. It will be my parting bow to the scientific world; and I flatter myself that the contribution will arouse intense interest in scientific circles, and that I shall have added a new and striking term to the medical vocabulary. I shall probably have the article completed in a fortnight's time—meanwhile, remember, mum's the word!"

One day, about a week after this conversation had taken place, I was returning to lunch after my usual morning's round of visiting, when, just as I turned the corner of Elton Place, I caught sight of a uniformed nurse tripping up the steps of number 52. I quickened my pace, thinking that it probably meant another visit for me, and determined to fortify the inner man by a hurried snack before setting out again. As I reached the door it was opened by Martha Brown, our housekeeper, pale, red-eyed, and incoherent. I gathered with some difficulty that Burton, while walking in the back garden about half an hour previously, had had an apoplectic seizure, and that Drs. Hughes and Stevens were in attendance. Just then Hughes came downstairs and turned with me into the consulting-room, where we were joined a few moments later by Stevens.

"Sad business, this," said Hughes. "I fear it is only the beginning of the end. Burton ought to have retired a year ago, as Stevens advised him."

"Right hemiplegia," chimed in Stevens in his staccato manner. "Pretty bad case, too—total aphemia—also agraphia—tried to write something—only scrawled a lot of rubbish. My best nurse is with him now—you have a look at him now and then—I'll be back in an hour or two."

He took his departure in his usual abrupt fashion, and shortly afterward Hughes left me with a murmured commiseration over the extra work and responsibility devolving on my shoulders.

I made my way to Burton's room, and was shocked at the change in his appearance. His whole right side was paralysed, and the dropping eyelid and wry mouth imparted a peculiar expression to his face. He was quite speechless, and, although he had tried to write with his left hand, owing to defective co-ordination he was unable to commit his thoughts to paper. I told the nurse that I would sit with him while she had her lunch; and as she left the room I picked up the sheet of paper on which the patient had attempted to convey his wishes. Immediately a light dawned on my comprehension. Small wonder that Hughes and Stevens had dismissed it as incoherent rubbish. Every line commenced with "Opistho-pisth—" and then trailed away into a scrawl in which no letters were decipherable.

"I understand what you mean," I said. "You are referring to your article on opisthophobia; you wish it sent off in time to appear in the next issue of the *Journal of Nervous Disease*?"

He nodded assent, and then his eyes filled with tears at his own helplessness. "Don't worry about it," I said. "Just to put your mind at ease I'll get the manuscript ready for the next post, and see that it goes to-night without fail."

I took Burton's bunch of keys from his chain. With his left hand he pointed out the required key; and guided by his nods, I opened a drawer in his dressing table which contained some of his private papers, including the MS. of the precious article. In the same drawer I found some large envelopes, in one of which I placed the MS.; and then in his presence I closed and addressed it. He smiled his thanks faintly, and the expression of uneasiness gave way to one of relief.

The nurse returned to the sick-room, and I left him with the parting injunction that he was not to worry, and an assurance that everything would be all right. I placed the envelope on the letter-rack in the hall, intending to post it myself at five o'clock, when the hours of consultation were over, and the waiting-room was empty of patients. By four o'clock I had seen the last patient, for some of Burton's special charges had gone away on learning that he was unable to see them that day. As I stepped out into the hall, I saw the nurse coming downstairs two steps at a time. "Come, at once," she said. "He's got a turn for the worse."

I went quickly up to Burton's room, and found him in a state of coma; his breathing slow and stertorous. I rang up Stevens, who arrived in a few minutes. He looked grave, and shook his head.

"As I feared," he muttered. "Fresh cerebral haemorrhage—absolutely comatose—probably all over in a few hours—poor old Burton—well! well!—such is life—and death."

He gave some directions to the nurse, and went off again, promising to look in later on. "Not that I can do anything," he concluded, "for I don't believe he will ever recover consciousness."

The sudden shock had unnerved me to a greater extent than I should have thought possible. It was a complete upset to my expectation. I had pictured to myself Burton gradually passing over all his patients to me, and retiring from practice in a few years' time. This sudden development, I reflected, was calculated to scare away a large number of our regular patients. I paced to and fro in the garden, and tried to think out my plans for the future; but my mind was too disturbed to follow any one line of thought for long. I wandered into the sick-room occasionally, and glanced at the unconscious man. There was no change in his condition. I turned into the dining-room and stood at the window looking up and down the street. The sight of a passing postman suddenly reminded me of a neglected duty! Burton's article had not been posted. The thought of my remissness, and the memory of poor Burton's anxiety, brought me a quick stab of compunction; but, on second thoughts, I reflected sadly that it mattered little now when it was posted; for even the proof-sheets would never gladden the eyes of the author; and it seemed to me better to hold it over until I should have the leisure to compose a suitable obituary notice, which might appear along with the article in a later issue of the journal. That act of procrastination, justifiable though it appeared at the moment, was the first step to my downfall. And yet I can solemnly aver that as I took the envelope from the rack, and placed it in a pigeon-hole of my roll-top desk, my conscience felt clear and my motives were innocent in the sight of heaven. Burton died that night.

A fortnight after the funeral, as I sat at my desk writing an obituary notice of Burton for the *Journal of Nervous Diseases*, and as I had just begun the enumeration of his published works and contributions, I laid down my pen for a moment and began to consider how I should introduce a reference to his now posthumous article on opisthophobia. I took the envelope out of its pigeon-hold, opened it, and read the manuscript through. I realise now that in so doing I had taken the second step on the way to destruction; but at the time I argued in this fashion: It was true that Burton's wish had been that no one should read it until it appeared in print; but, had he foreseen the situation that had arisen, he would doubtless have given me permission to do so; especially as I was about to make particular reference to the article in the notice upon which I was engaged. Besides, as though to soothe any prickings of conscience, I found that the article was incomplete. It ended rather abruptly, and there were a few spaces left here and there for the insertion of references. Evidently Burton had intended to put the finishing touches to it when revising the proofs. On the face of it, then, it remained for me to make it as complete as I could, and to append a note explaining the necessity for so doing, and the consequent delay in forwarding it for publication.

No sooner had I, in perfect good faith, decided upon this course, than a great wave of temptation rose up and smote me with a force beneath which my whole moral being reeled. I struggled against it for a moment, wavered—and fell.

From that day to this I have failed to account for it satisfactorily to myself, and I cannot hope that I could ever succeed in putting forward an explanation of my conduct which would satisfy others. I wish it to be clearly understood that I am not endeavouring to defend an act which was indefensible; I am only trying to explain it. The fact is that I am so accustomed to analysing the mental processes of others, in my professional capacity, that I cannot refrain from analysing my own. It was only after Burton's death that I began to realise the extent to which our combined practice depended upon the reputation of my colleague. For years I had done the lion's share of the work; I was lacking neither in knowledge nor in experience—only in reputation. I had written nothing beyond a few short notes of cases; I had had no time for writing; but Burton had published three books which were standard works, and for years scarcely a month passed without something from his pen appearing in some of the medical journals. Patients quickly get wind of these facts; and especially patients of the class on which our practice depended. Morbid-minded hypochondriacs who pore over the medical books exposed for sale on the second-hand bookstalls could not fail to come across copies of Burton's *Lectures on Mental Disease*. Since his death, the number of my patients had steadily decreased; and when, within a few days of that event, another specialist, fresh from his studies in Vienna, actually set up a rival practice half a dozen doors off, my consulting-room became practically deserted. Here was an opportunity of winning a reputation without further delay. Burton's was established for all time; the posthumous fame accruing to him from his last contribution on the small pebble to an already monumental cairn. On the other hand, it would be the foundation-stone of mine. My imagination already conjured up a paragraph in the future editions of the *Dictionary of Medicine*, beginning: "Opisthophobia, also known as Crawley's Disease, because first described by Dr. Robert Crawley, of Dublin, etc. etc."

I finished the obituary notice without making any reference to the article before me. The article itself I carefully locked up in my desk, and then I went out for a stroll.

For a whole month I devoted my evenings to the completion of the article. I verified and supplied references; altered the phraseology in places where it was obviously Burtonian; and, having by studious perusal of the MS. rendered myself thoroughly conversant with the case, I ventured with a considerable amount of confidence to complete the unfinished sentence with which the MS. ended, and even to continue the subject for several pages in which I advanced theories of my own. Finally, I copied out the whole article in my own hand-writing; consigned Burton's MS. to the flames, and sent on my revised version for publication.

It created a great sensation in medical circles, and for fully twelve months afterwards a correspondence was carried on in the columns of the various journals of Psychiatry. I was almost overwhelmed with questions on the subject; but I had so thoroughly mastered the details of the case that I had no difficulty in replying. I became famous. My practice grew rapidly, and I amassed a considerable fortune in a very short time. It was no uncommon occurrence for me to receive a fee of one hundred guineas as a consultant; while publishers eagerly bought up the copyright of my books. My reputation was assured; owing to my dishonest act I flourished like a green bay tree.

My mind has derived a certain amount of relief from the reflection that I have succeeded in making a full confession of my crime—for crime I must call it—and that, painful though the process has been, I have not flinched at the stern necessity of laying bare the secrets of my inmost soul. A still more painful duty, however, lies before me; and I pray that as I have been enabled to confess my crime I may also have the necessary fortitude to record its punishment. There are two considerations which help to brace me for the task; in the first place, as I have already stated, a knowledge of the fact that my punishment has been grievous may induce my many judges to temper their condemnation with some modicum of mercy; and, secondly, the value to the profession of the record of a rare case, noted by one who has filled the two-fold capacity of patient and medical adviser, may to some extent atone for my fault.

Towards the end of February last, I had a sharp attack of influenza; and it was while convalescing that the first symptom of my disease manifested itself. I was sitting in my study revising the proof-sheets of the final chapters of my work on "Hereditary Neuroses", when it became necessary for me to consult my copy of the *Medical Journal* which I had left in the dining-room earlier in the evening. My housekeeper had retired, and the ground floor was in darkness; but I knew exactly where the journal was lying, and so I descended without a light. I had scarcely entered the dining-room when a vague and indescribable terror seized me. My reasoning powers completely forsook me, and I fled incontinently upstairs to the study, and burst into the room shaking in every limb, my heart thumping against my ribs like a sledgehammer, and a cold perspiration be-dewing my forehead. I sank into a chair and drank off a glass of brandy and soda which Martha, according to her custom, had placed on the study table before she retired. The stimulant pulled me together quickly, and as soon as I had collected my wits I began to laugh at my absurd conduct. I attributed my nervousness to the after-effects of influenza, and lighting my bedroom candle I went downstairs again and secured the journal. I went to bed that night determined to keep earlier hours, and to avoid perambulating in the dark until my nervous system had recovered its normal tone. I adhered to my determination, and after a week or so I had completely dismissed the matter from my mind; when one night as I entered my bedroom, candlestick in hand, the draught from the open window extinguished the light.

Immediately the same feeling of terror swooped down upon me with intensified force. I strove in vain to keep my presence of mind. I felt as though all the unknown horror of the powers of darkness were stretching forth their fearful hands to clutch at me from behind. I staggered back against the wall and faced the empty room, and the feeling of protection afforded by the touch of the solid wall next my back caused the sudden wave of terror to subside sufficiently to enable me to fumble for a match and relight my candle; but there was no sleep for me that night. I returned to my study and tried to think the situation over. I lighted the gas, seated myself in the armchair, and began to consider my case as calmly as I could. There was little use in trying to hide from myself the unpalatable truth; avenging Nemesis had tracked me down; there was not the faintest shadow of doubt about the diagnosis; what the prognosis might be time alone would tell, but so far as I could judge the outlook was serious. One thing was absolutely certain—I was suffering from Opisthophobia!

What was to be done? I should have to treat my own case as best I could. Even if I travelled to Vienna and consulted the most eminent specialist in psychiatry, I should be told that there was only one man living who was an authority on the subject, *viz.*, Crawley, of Dublin! When I thought of the irony of it all I could hardly restrain myself from giving vent to shrieks of sardonic laughter.

I paced restlessly to and fro all night, until the day dawned, and then, wearied out, I sank into a chair and slept. For a month after this I ran no risks. I never went out after dusk, and I slept with a light in my room. Then I ventured to experiment on myself. One night when Martha Brown was about to turn out the hall gas, I called down to her that she should leave it burning, and that I would see to it myself before I went to bed.

Fortifying myself with a powerful nerve stimulant and walking down with a certain amount of assurance, I boldly turned out the light. No sooner did I find myself standing in the centre of the dark hall than the old terror smote me once more. A cry of horror escaped my lips, and rushing for the staircase I pressed my back against the wall and began to sidle my way upstairs.

Martha came running down in her dressing gown to know what had happened. I muttered some feeble excuse about knocking my knee against a hall chair; but I could see by her expression that she believed the cry she had heard to be the result of other than physical pain.

Six weeks later I made a second and last experiment. It happened in this way: I met Stevens in consultation one morning, and as we came away from the patient's house he remarked that I did not look quite fit. He advised me to give up work and go away for a change of air. " 'Of making of books there is no end'," he quoted, " 'and much study is a weariness of the flesh.' Take my advice and drop it for the present—no use in knocking yourself up—can't afford to lose a prominent specialist, you know."

As we parted at my door-steps he wrung from me a promise to dine with him on the following evening in company with some bachelor friends. I arrived at Stevens' fully half an hour before dinner-time; partly in order to get there by daylight, and partly because I entertained a faint hope that I might take my courage in both hands and make a clean breast of my trouble to him in strict confidence. Once there, however, my courage failed me, and I chatted with him on various other subjects until the other guests arrived. During the course of the evening my spirits rose. I actually found myself laughing at the witticisms that were being bandied about at the table, and I enjoyed a game of cards afterwards. My carriage came for me at half-past ten, and I manoeuvred so that Stevens came out with me and stood chatting with me for a few seconds at the carriage door. The blaze of light which streamed from the open door of Stevens' house dispelled all fear of an attack, but as soon as the carriage drove away through the dimly lighted streets I began to expect a seizure at any moment. I felt fairly secure so long as I kept my back well pressed against the carriage cushions, but when we stopped at my door, and I saw that the hall gas was turned down to a feeble glimmer, I became so demoralised that I actually feigned intoxication, so that Simpson, my coachman, might assist me up to my bedroom without asking questions. To such a depth had I fallen that I was reduced to lying to my housekeeper and shamming drunkenness to my coachman! I looked forward with relief to the long summer days when the dreaded hours of darkness should be few, and I could go for long walks into the country. Nothing that Stevens could say would induce me to go away for a holiday; I dared not travel and risk a seizure in a strange hotel, where I might be taken for a lunatic.

‡

The summer came but it did not bring with it the relief that I had expected. I discovered to my intense dismay that the attacks of terror were no longer confined to the hours of darkness, but that I was liable to a seizure even in the daylight unless I sat in such a position that there was no empty space at my back which could harbour the dread Fiend that walked behind. This discovery decided my course of action for the future. I retired from practice, refused to see any visitors, and became a perfect recluse.

‡

It is now December, but I shall never live to see Christmas. I feel that the end is near, and I can almost welcome it. Whatever fate the future holds in store for me, no more grievous retribution can await me than that which I have already suffered for the past few months. I have taken up my quarters in the study, and have not left it for more than a few minutes at mid-day during the last three weeks. I can get no sleep. I have tried all the soporific drugs in the *British Pharmocopœia*, but they seem to have lost their effect. My appetite has failed, and I am growing daily weaker. My housekeeper believes that I am insane, but she has given up suggesting medical advice since I told her that I knew I was suffering from an incurable complaint. I believe it is for the sake of old times that she continues to remain with me.

‡

I never was at any time very religiously inclined, yet as the end draws near there are thoughts that will arise. Only this morning while turning over aimlessly the leaves of an old Black-Letter Psalter—one of Burton's rare editions which he loved to collect—I came across the sentence: "*Non timebis a timore nocturne*": but on glancing back over the context I found that the passage occurred in a Psalm beginning: "*Qui habitat in adjutorio Altissimi; in protectione Dei cœli commorabitur*"—and I have forfeited all claim to the Divine protection.

I cannot endure these frequent fits of terror much longer. I must finish this document somehow, although my hand has grown so shaky that I can scarcely write legibly. With the exception of an annuity to Martha Brown, I have bequeathed all my personal estate to the Trustees of the National Hospital for Nervous Diseases.

(Signed) ROBERT CRAWLEY.
December 14, 18—

The Homing Bone

Professor David Gillespie was a distinguished anatomist. It is scarcely necessary to add that he was a Scotsman; or has not a wise Providence ordained that the principal products of Caledonia shall be marine engineers, metaphysicians, and anatomists? Equally brilliant on what are technically known as the "hard" and "soft" parts of the human frame, he was particularly strong on the subject of the skeleton; and to hear him lecture on the petrous portion of the temporal bone was a revelation to the unsophisticated first-year students of medicine. In the lecture theatre he would stand at the rostrum, of a morning, and taking a bone for his text, he would hold forth for a full hour. Common "grinders" could point out foramina and muscle-insertion well enough for examination purposes; but their instruction was dry and uninteresting. In Gillspie's hands a bone became a thing of beauty. His lecture was not a lecture; it was not a sermon; it was an oration. He would wax eloquent as he went along, and his enthusiasm was infectious. Not infrequently, when his peroration closed with some apposite quotation from the poets, a spontaneous burst of applause went up from the crowded benches; and students, as they wended their way to pastures new, would remark to one another: "Man, but Gillespie's just great!"

Professor Gillespie came of Highland Gaelic stock; a stock which is far from materialistic; and his grandmother was reputed to have possessed the gift of "second sight". Many a time young Davy had shuddered as he listened, by the fire of the crofter's cottage, where he first saw the light, to the weird, uncanny tales of the Highlands; but five years' hard work at the Edinburgh School of Medicine had knocked the nonsense out of him in more ways than one. Now, at the age of fifty-four, one of the leading anatomists of Europe, he could afford to bestow an indulgent smile on the narrator of tales pertaining to the supernatural. A man who, for twenty years, has spent most of his waking hours in the atmosphere of the Dissecting-room, is almost as much at home with the dead as with the living. His stock-in-trade, so to speak, being corpses, the creepiest story about "corpse-candles" naturally leaves him unmoved. Yet the fear of the supernatural is so deeply ingrained in human beings, and the stories heard in boyhood days sink so deeply into the subliminal self, that the acquired scepticism of later years is, after all, the merest veneer, which may vanish in a moment; if only circumstances arise, in which a sufficiently strong appeal is made to those hereditary instincts and pre-historic beliefs that slumber beneath the surface.

So much, by way of preface to the secret history of the curious happenings which led to Gillespie's resignation of his Chair of Anatomy, and his retirement into private life; a step which astonished all who heard of it, for he was regarded as being but at the zenith of his powers. I now tell the tale as it was told to me by Cochrane, who heard it from the lips of Gillespie himself.

When the British Medical Association held its annual conference in Dublin, Gillespie was invited to preside over the Anatomical Section; and his address at the opening meeting of the section was as brilliant as might have been expected from one of his reputation. The conference over, Gillespie devoted his time to sight-seeing. He spent a day visiting the Cathedrals, and, in the afternoon, he prowled about the quays and the back streets of the city. Half an hour was given up to viewing the vaults of St. Michan's, with its celebrated mummies, and crossing the Metal Bridge he wended his way through Cook Street, that home of undertakers, where every shop resounds to the stroke of the coffin-maker's hammer.

Having passed through this gruesome quarter, he wandered further afield, until he came upon the old church of St. Walburgh's. The ground about the church had long been closed to burials, and he found some workmen engaged in levelling the churchyard. The tombstones had been removed and arranged along the churchyard wall; for, since the inscriptions they bore were no longer legible, they had served their purpose, and were mere cumberers of the ground. During the levelling process some relics of mortality had become uncovered, and in one corner there lay a jumble of odd assortments of skulls and some large bones.

Gillespie's professional eye detected, amid the heap, a splendid specimen in a perfect state of preservation. It was a thigh-bone, or as an anatomist would more accurately describe it, a left femur; that of an adult man, for, by the trained eye, the sterner sex can be distinguished even in the bony structures. The professor coveted the bone, and foresaw in it the material for an interesting and instructive paper. He had no qualms of conscience about securing it; only, in deference to any susceptibilities on the part of the Irish workmen, he did so quite unostentatiously, and walked away with the coveted femur concealed beneath his overcoat.

Arrived at his lodgings, he stowed it in his bedroom until after dinner; when he proceeded to brush away the adherent earth from the bone with a clothes-brush, and settled down to gloat over his treasure. From the great length of the femur, and the powerfully developed trochanters, he deduced the fact that the man who had owned it must have been an exceptionally tall and muscular individual; and the professor fell to wondering whether the said individual had been an Irishman or one of the old Norse stock whose descendants among the Dubliners retain somewhat of the Viking characteristics. He sat in his dressing-gown until eleven o'clock, and strove to visualise the appearance which the owner of the bone must have presented in life; then he yawned sleepily, and dropped the femur into his portmanteau, lest he might forget it in his hurry to catch the morning boat, he tumbled into bed and fell fast asleep.

His sleep had not lasted for long when he was visited by a horribly vivid dream. In his dream he seemed to be awakened by the sound of knocking at his bedroom door. Before he had time to say "Come in!" the door opened, and four skeletons entered, carrying a coffin on their bony shoulders. They deposited their burden on two chairs beside his bed, and stood like waiting mutes. Suddenly the lid of the coffin flew open, and its occupant, a tall skeleton, sat up and pointed first at the professor, and then to its own lower limbs. Following the gesture, Gillespie looked and saw that the left femur was missing. Still sitting up in the coffin, the tall skeleton leaned forward towards the bed and clutched the professor by the throat with a vice-like grip of its bony fingers.

Gillespie gasped for breath, gave a strangled scream, and woke up in a fright. It took some little time for him to realise his surroundings. He sat up in bed to find his heart palpitating violently, his brow wet with perspiration, and about his scalp a curious sensation associated in the lay mind with the phenomenon known as "the hair standing on end". It was decidedly a novel experience for the professor, for he boasted that he never dreamed dreams, or that if he did, they were so unimportant, that his waking moments contained no recollection of them.

The explanation was perfectly simple, he told himself. During the conference his meals had been more irregular than they would have been at home. Some of the dinners, too, were more elaborate than those to which he was normally accustomed. Why, he wondered, could not a party of grave and learned scientists foregather without over-eating and over-drinking like a lot of schoolboys at a picnic? Then the material of his dream had been supplied by his afternoon saunter through that extraordinary street of coffin-shops, and the bone purloined from the churchyard completed the tale.

Yet, in that dark room, in the small hours of the morning there were stirrings of the hereditary fears—the fear of the dark and the fear of the dead; and he fell to moralising over the fact that Providence had for some reason or other seen fit to endow the human scalp with a set of *"erector pili"* or hair-raising muscles, and the further curious fact that that particular set of muscles could only be called into play by supernatural (or superstitious) terrors. Did not the pious Aeneas' hair stand on end at the apparition of his beloved dead wife, Creusa? But the professor's classics were decidedly rusty, and while attempting in vain to complete the line *"Obstupui, steteruntque comae"*—he fell asleep once more.

However, he was not destined to enjoy his resumed slumber for long. The ill dream was repeated with variations. Once more the door opened, the four skeletons entered, bearing a coffin which they placed on chairs by the bedside; but this time the lid did not fly open. Instead, the professor found his gaze directed by the bony forefingers of the skeletons to the name-plate on the coffin-lid; and, to his horror, he saw the name of the deceased was set forth as DAVID GILLESPIE.

While he still gazed in horror-stricken silence, a troupe of skeletons came crowding into the room, and circled round his bed in a dance of death, their bones rattling like castanets, and their grinning jaws gnashing as though chanting a hymn of hate. Closer and closer they circled, until one gigantic skeleton halted, and raising an enormous thigh-bone, aimed a stunning blow straight at the professor's head. Gillespie instinctively put up one arm to ward off the impending blow, and the effort awoke him.

This time he was indignant. He had refused several offers of hospitality from Dublin hosts, preferring to select quiet lodgings for himself. That was one of his idiosyncrasies; for he strongly objected to sitting up into the small hours, smoking and talking "shop"; and experience of many Medical Congresses had proved such dissipation to be the normal sequel to accepting the hospitality of professional colleagues. And now here he was faring no better, or rather worse. Confound it all! His digestion must be completely upset. If only he had strolled into the country, instead of through those unhealthy back streets adjoining the Liffey. His head felt decidedly queer, too, and he reflected that it was probably the queer feeling which had coloured the finale of his second nightmare. Could it be something more serious than indigestion?

Gillespie had read somewhere that Chinese physicians attached great importance to the prognostic interpretation of their patients' dreams. Did the curious variant by which he distinctly saw his own name inscribed on the coffin-lid portend a dangerous illness? Such gruesome visions reminded him of the creepy tales heard in his childhood days. His grandmother, who was popularly credited with "second sight", used to tell of how she had seen a coffin, with her husband's name on it, carried past in the moonlight, three days before he died.

One story recalled another. There were stirrings in the subliminal mind. As a boy he firmly believed in ghosts. Why exactly had he lost that belief? Like the Missionary, in one of Robert Louis Stevenson's fables, he began to think that after all there might be something in it. The French called ghosts *"revenants"*, folk who came back. Came back for what? If he told his dream to any of the old wives in his native village they would roundly assert that the dead Irishman, or Dane, as the case might be, had come back for the femur that had been stolen from the churchyard. This introduced another train of thought; consecrated earth. Yes, the bones which had served him for purposes of lecturing for the past twenty years, were bones that had been taken from the dissecting-room, macerated, and bleached. They had never been interred; had never lain in consecrated earth. Should he, in deference to sentiment, restore the femur to the churchyard, after first making a neat sketch and recording the exact measurements?

Needless to say, Gillespie in his normal waking mood, and in broad daylight, would never have soliloquised in this strain; but, as I have already hinted, the dark brings back forgotten fears and scruples, and the professor was by no means in a normal mood. His thoughts were running on this long unused track for some minutes, when he dozed asleep again. But did he? For that is a question which no man living can answer—not even the intelligent reader. Gillespie stoutly denied that he did. Cochrane declared that he only dreamt he did not; that, in point of fact, what followed was part of the same dream, and that it was a part of the dream to dream that he was awake.

Be that as it may, let us abide by Gillespie's version for the present. He was (let us premise) still awake, and following out this line of thought, when he heard a dull knocking sound in the room. It was a muffled tapping, repeated at regular intervals, and appeared to proceed from the closed portmanteau which lay on the floor close to the dressing-table. Although the room was quite dark, Gillespie instinctively glanced in the direction from which the sound proceeded, and as he did so he became aware of a faint, hazy luminosity of rectangular form. The luminosity increased in brilliance, until it became quite evidently the outline of the portmanteau, with a distinct view of its interior, as though it had been placed against a fluorescent screen, under the action of exceptionally powerful Röntgen Rays; and the object which stood out most clearly, as in an actual skiagraph, was the purloined femur. So sharply was it defined that it appeared to impress a photograph of itself on Gillespie's brain; and then the fluorescence died away, and the room was plunged in darkness again.

By this time, the professor was (so he asserted to Cochrane) as wide awake as ever he had been in his life; his every sense strung to the highest pitch of expectation; but thenceforward he was obliged to depend solely upon his sense of hearing for information as to subsequent events. He distinctly heard, he alleged, a noise as of someone fumbling with the catch of the portmanteau; the click with which it opened; and a dull thudding sound, as of someone walking in the room with a wooden leg or crutch. Next, his bedroom door swung ajar, and the someone or something stumped slowly down stairs and along the matting of the hall. The front door opened slightly—enough to send a current of air sweeping up the stairs and into the bedroom—and closed again noiselessly.

All this time, Gillespie was mentally alert, and experienced no abnormal sensations, except for a tense feeling about the head, and a curious inability, or even willingness, to move or speak. Then came a blank in consciousness, and he remembered no more until he awoke to find it broad daylight.

A knock at his bedroom door heralded the arrival of no more supernatural a visitant than the maid-of-all-work with his boots and shaving-water. He rose with something of an effort, and the act of stooping for his boots and hot water caused his head to throb violently; while the singing in his ears almost deafened him. But, like Macbeth, the terrors of the night being gone he felt himself a man again; and he was in a humour to explain his present, as well as his past, experience in terms of materialistic philosophy. Dyspepsia;

that was the explanation in a nutshell. Dyspepsia, coupled with a restless night.

Shaved and dressed, he hastened to complete his packing, and opened his portmanteau to stow away his shaving tackle and toilet brushes. As he opened it, he recollected with a smile how he had debated with himself in the watches of the night the advisability of returning the stolen bone to the churchyard; but he decided that such an action would be a concession to a temporary aberration of superstitious weakness; better keep it as a memento of his visit to Dublin.

Now if Professor Gillespie had been an untidy, unmethodical man, this story would not have been told; but the fact remains that nothing would do him but to empty the contents of the portmanteau on the floor, in order to pack away all his belongings neatly. And then it was that he made the discovery that caused him to abandon the idea of catching that day's boat, and sent him instead to consult Cochrane in Merrion Square. He discovered that the bone was missing!

It was only when he had thoroughly satisfied himself that it really was missing, by replacing the contents of the portmanteau, article by article, repeating the process several times, and making a thorough inventory of the objects in the room, that he decided that there was something wrong. Had he at this time of life begun to indulge in day-dreams, or was he the victim of hallucinations? He would have sworn in any court of law that he had conveyed the bone to his room the night before, brushed it clean, and placed it in his portmanteau. Was that waking experience on a par with the visions of the night? Was he taking leave of his senses?

He toyed with his breakfast, and informing his landlady that he had changed his mind, and intended to leave by the evening boat instead, he made a last desperate effort to regain his normal bearings. Mid-day found him once more standing in the churchyard of St. Walburgh's. The workmen were still engaged in levelling the surface, but one of their number was re-interring the heap of bones which had been laid aside in the corner. Only one portion of skull and a few long bones were left uncovered; and among the latter, in precisely the identical position which it occupied when Gillespie's eyes first lightened upon it, was the great left femur!

There was no mistaking it; for, apart from the size and abnormal development, it was as free from churchyard mould as though it had been freshly washed and dusted. Instead of throwing light on the subject, this only complicated matters still further. What was the meaning of it all? His head sang and throbbed so much that it was with difficulty that he made his way as far as his lodging.

In the afternoon he went to Cochrane's, and sent in his card. It had the opposite effect to that which he intended; for, instead of seeing him immediately, Cochrane kept him waiting until he had seen the last of his patients, hoping to settle down to a long chat on subjects arising out of the Conference.

When Gillespie's turn did eventually come, and he had finished relating his strange experiences, both in dreaming and waking states, Cochrane put to him a few questions, and set about a thorough examination. Every medical consultant has his own particular fad; and Cochrane's fad was blood-pressure. Once he adjusted the sphygmomanometer, and found that the professor's blood-pressure stood at 210, he cared nothing about reflexes or pupil-reaction. Blood-pressure explained everything, and in Cochrane's opinion the whole matter was simple.

Gillespie, like most anatomists and other specialists, had forgotten all he ever knew about the ordinary practice of medicine. He thought that, so long as he was oblivious to the flight of time, his arteries were in a similar state. As a matter of fact, they were prematurely senile and sclerosed from the routine of his life and the mental pre-occupation which had caused him to neglect precautions suitable for a man of middle age. It was highly probable that the bursting of a small arteriole in the brain had given rise to the sensation of a "stroke", metamorphosed into a blow aimed at his head by the skeleton of his dream fancy.

The upshot of the consultation was that Gillespie was prevailed upon, under stress of warnings as to the serious consequences of disobedience, to resign his Chair of Anatomy and retire from public life. He took a quiet bungalow in his native air, and persevered in the gentle exercise treatment prescribed by Cochrane; but rest had come too late, for he was carried off by a severe stroke within seven months of his resignation; so that Cochrane's diagnosis was not very far wrong after all.

I first heard Cochrane tell this story at a clinical lecture on arterio-sclerosis; but at the time he mentioned no names. It was since I qualified that I wormed the whole tale out of him, with full particulars, as well as he could remember them. Still, blood-pressure will not explain everything; and I firmly believe that Gillespie did remove the femur from the churchyard, and stow it in his portmanteau. To my mind, the only question that remains unanswered is this: "How did it find its way back again?"

Professor Danvers' Disappearance

"I think the most curious case that ever came before my notice in the whole course of my career was that of the disappearance of Professor Danvers." The speaker was Ellingham, a successful private detective, who was one of the guests at a bachelor dinner-party, in Christmas week, at Colonel Spence's place. When cigars had been lighted up we started swopping yarns, and finally we drew Ellingham.

"Danvers was a distinguished Orientalist who lived in a small detached house near Westcliffe-on-Sea. He was a Fellow of several learned societies, and spoke five or six Indian dialects fluently. In addition to his Oriental studies, he dabbled in the occult, and contributed articles from time to time to the *Occult Review* and the *Journal of the Society for Psychical Research*. His house was a rendezvous for Orientals of all sorts; in fact the majority of his visitors wore either a turban or a fez. It was even rumoured locally that he had on one occasion entertained a Mahatma from Tibet.

"Except for a stroll before bedtime he might be said to have lived in his study on the ground-floor of the house. From morning to night he pored over manuscripts ranging from Prakrit dramas, written on parchment, to the sacred Tripiṭakas of the Buddhists, inscribed on palm-leaves. He was a recognised authority on theosophical literature, and could discourse very learnedly about reincarnations, avatars, astral bodies, and planes. Indeed, his extraordinary brilliancy in the domain of Asiatic lore was accounted for, in the opinion of English theosophists, by the theory that in former incarnations he had been a Brahmin or a Yogi.

"His disappearance would leave a noticeable blank in the learned world; but the life in Westcliffe would have kept the even tenor of its way, had it not been for the curious circumstances connected with his manner of vanishing from human ken. 'Vanish' is the only word fit to describe his departure. One evening he received by post a letter which seemed to exercise a disturbing influence over him. According to his housekeeper he was more *distrait* than usual, and left his meal almost untasted. He retired to his study, as usual, leaving his dinner unfinished. The following morning he left for London by an early train, returning the same day about six o'clock. He refused dinner, explaining that he was about to engage in an important psychical experiment which required as one condition of success that the experimenter should be fasting for several hours.

" 'By the way, Mrs. Ebbitt,' remarked Danvers to his housekeeper, as she was on the point of proceeding to clear away the dinner-table, 'if any visitor should call, it is important that I should not be disturbed before nine. As a matter of fact, I am expecting a Hindu gentleman to-night at that hour; but, in case that he should arrive before then, please ask him to sit on the hall lounge until I open the study door. He will not mind waiting a few minutes.'

"At five minutes to nine the hall doorbell rang, and Mrs. Ebbitt opened the door to find a dark-complexioned man dressed in European clothes, except for a turban on his head. She admitted him to the hall, and requested him to wait until the professor was ready to receive him. Just as she was re-entering the dining-room she heard the study door open; the waiting Hindu, talking volubly in Hindustani, passed through; the voice of the professor was heard by her to say in English: 'When did you start from Bombay?' and then the study door closed once more.

"Half an hour later, Mrs. Ebbitt, who was again in the dining-room laying the table for supper, heard the study door open. There was a brief dialogue in the doorway; the professor said: 'You will excuse my not showing you to the door. Please find your own way out. Good-bye!' At this the housekeeper stepped out into the hall and opened the street-door for the foreign gentleman. He passed out into the night, and Mrs. Ebbitt returned to the dining-room to complete the supper arrangements. At ten o'clock she knocked at the study door, and, as there was no reply, she opened the door slightly and called to the professor: 'I am retiring now, sir, and I've left the cold roast on the table if you'd care for a bit of supper.'

"Still no reply. She entered the study. The professor was not to be seen. Her blood ran cold as she glanced towards his armchair which was drawn up to his roll-top desk. A limp mass lay inertly in the chair. She checked a scream of terror. Had the foreigner murdered him? But no, she had heard his voice speaking as he closed the study door, and the foreigner had not entered the study a second time. Perhaps the professor had fainted from fasting so long? But this was no ordinary faint. There was something gruesome about the mass in the chair. Screwing up her courage she came closer, and made a very curious discovery. The chair held nothing but the professor's clothes, and on the floor in front of the chair were his boots and socks! Had he suddenly become insane and stripped himself of his garments to rush madly out of the French window of the study and wander round the roads in a state of nature?

"The police must be immediately informed. Donning her bonnet and cloak she went off for assistance. She had not far to go before she met a constable, who accompanied her to the house. The constable entered the study and examined the clothes. Then he searched every room in the house, looked in the bath and under it, returned to the study again and stared at the clothes. He agreed that there was some likelihood of Mrs. Ebbitt's third hypothesis being the correct one. His exact words were: 'Swelp me if the pore old geezer ain't gone barmy and took to the countryside in his buff!'

"The policeman went off to report the matter to head-quarters. Twenty-four hours passed, but there was no trace of Danvers to be found. This was strange, on the hypothesis of his sudden lunacy; for even a distinguished Orientalist could hardly expect to be pardoned the eccentricity of walking abroad minus his garments; and no one had caught so much as a glimpse of a nude figure anywhere. The superintendent of police closely examined the heap of clothes for bloodstains, but could not find any. However, close examination revealed a bizarre feature which had at first escaped notice. *The professor had not undressed!* At any rate that was the impression given by a close scrutiny. None of the garments was unbuttoned or undone, as would have been the case even in a hurried undressing. His tie was still fastened around his collar, which was studded to his shirt, and so on down to the boots from which the tops of his socks protruded, for the boots had not been unlaced! If Danvers' body had slowly melted away and sunk into the ground as he sat in his armchair, then his clothes would have been left in the precise condition in which they had been found. And, silly though it may appear, when the papers got hold of this circumstance, there were many who held that that was what had actually happened.

"Writers in occult and spiritualistic journals explained that Danvers, being a clever student of Oriental Yogiism, and a natural psychic of great powers, had succeeded in de-ma-terialising his body, and he was now existing on the astral plane. He had announced to his housekeeper his intention of trying a very important psychical experiment, and he had evidently succeeded beyond his expectations. Whether he intended to materialise again must now remain matter for conjecture; for, as one correspondent in *Light* pointed out, the disarrangement of his clothing by so many unimaginative non-psychics, like police constables and detectives, would render the condition impossible for a return to normal.

"On one point both the theosophists and the spiritualists agreed, and that was that it was exceedingly doubtful if Professor Danvers would ever be seen again on the earth plane. In other words, he was to be considered dead and buried for practical purposes.

"This is where I came into the case. Presumption of death is sometimes a ticklish legal point. Of course, if Danvers had gone on an expedition to a cannibal island, or if he had been last seen flying seawards in an aeroplane, his disappearance would create a strong presumption of death; but courts of law have not yet recognised the existence of astral planes or de-materialisations. Danvers held an insurance policy with the National Life Company for £5,000, and, although his next-of-kin had not been discovered, the company asked me to investigate the mystery of his disappearance.

"I called at the house and examined the study and its contents, noting the curious condition of the garments to which I have already referred. In the open roll-top desk, at which the Professor had been seated on that fateful evening, I found manuscripts in many different Eastern languages, letters from the secretaries of various learned societies, and one letter bearing the Bombay post-mark. It was an envelope containing a small scrap of rice-paper, no larger than a visiting card. On the piece of paper was drawn in Indian ink a rude symbol of the Swastika surmounted by crossed daggers, and, underneath, ran a series of small circles and semi-circles.

"I cross-examined the housekeeper. She recognised the letter from Bombay as the missive which caused the Professor's unusual agitation; for it was the only letter to arrive by the afternoon post on the day in question. She could not say if she had ever seen the foreign gentleman who had called on the evening of Professor Danvers' disappearance. To her eyes all dark gentlemen were very much alike. She would go so far, however, as to say that she thought there was something familiar about his figure and gait. She told in detail all she remembered about Danvers' movements since the receipt of the letter; his trip to London, and so on, as I have already told you.

"I inquired if she had noticed anything missing from the house. Yes, she had noticed that the Gladstone bag which the Professor had taken with him to London was no longer to be seen. Asked if he had the bag when he returned from London, she replied that he had it in his hand when he entered the study that evening. Could the Hindu visitor have removed it? No, she remembered distinctly that he carried nothing but an umbrella.

"There was nothing further to be learnt at Westcliffe; so I returned to London, bringing with me the mysterious drawing on rice-paper. That evening I submitted the paper to a competent Orientalist, and inquired the significance of the strange circles and semi-circles. It turned out that what I, in my ignorance, took to be mathematical drawing, were letters of the Pali alphabet. The writing was a single word—PARINIBBANA, which the Orientalist explained as meaning 'passing over to Nirvana', a Buddhist euphemism for death.

"The mystery was still baffling, but I thought I saw a glimpse of daylight. Not being an Oriental or a theosophist or a spiritualist, I did not for a moment accept the de-materialisation theory. I felt convinced that Danvers' body had not thawed and dissolved into a dew. The only doubt remaining in my mind was whether there was foul play or not. One very substantial clue I found in the disappearance of the Gladstone bag. Of course, when I handed over my slip of rice-paper to the police, and the journalists got wind of it, the occult devotees were jubilant. They were more persuaded than ever that the missing man was a fully developed Yogi, who had passed to Nirvana by a process of de-materialisation.

"Unfortunately, there was one clue which failed me. It transpired that the missing man kept no account with any of the banks; yet, I felt certain that if I could have tested this source of information I should have found that a considerable sum of money would be found missing also. I paid another visit to Westcliffe. The safe in the study where the Professor had been wont to keep his cash had been opened by a workman sent down by the firm of manufacturers. It was empty, and this fact tallied with my own theory.

"A further conversation with Mrs. Ebbitt revealed that among the many visitors who had called in the interval there was one who expressed great disappointment, since he had come all the way from Bombay to see Danvers. She happened to mention as curious that the last visitor to see him on the evening of his disappearance evidently came from Bombay also; because she had heard that the Professor ask: 'When did you start from Bombay?' At this the visitor perceptibly brightened and departed smiling.

"I now had my clues complete. I advised the insurance company to fight presumption of death, tooth and nail, and they did so successfully; and although Danvers is now missing many years the policy has not been paid. For one thing it has never been claimed."

"But what became of Danvers?" asked our host.

"I will tell you what I have good reason to think became of him," replied Ellingham. "In his early days, in India, Danvers entered thoroughly into native life and customs, so as to learn to think in the various dialects which he mastered. He went so far as to join a secret society, the membership of which had been hitherto confined to natives in India. As years went on, the development of the Swaraj movement reached a pitch when Danvers, as an Englishman, felt that he must break with the society. Then came the death-warning conveyed by the mystic word Parinibbana. He knew that the ordinary method for dealing with traitors to the society was for a member to visit him and offer him the choice between swallowing a pill containing a powerful alkaloid poison which left no trace that could be detected at an autopsy, or taking his chance of death by more violent means. That the messenger with the poison pill would call soon after the receipt of the letter was certain. There was no escape in any part of the British Empire; or in the world for that matter; so widespread were the toils of the Swastika-Prabandh.

"Now, in India, strange things are believed—possibly because there strange things happen. It was one of the traditions of the society that a certain Yogi who had been sentenced to death had dematerialised his body, so that, when the messenger reached him, nothing was to be found but a loin-cloth lying under the tree where he usually sat, and some iron armlets which could not be removed from his body during life, because he had worn them from boyhood, and they had partly bitten into his flesh.

"This is only surmise on my part; but I have been assured by an Orientalist that such tales are on record in Indian folk-lore, and they are readily believed. That was why the society adopted the word meaning 'passing to Nirvana' instead of the ordinary word for death. Adepts were supposed to be above mortality in the accepted sense. This gave Danvers the idea of feigning de-materialisation. Taking his empty bag to London, he returned with a suit of clothes, a pair of boots, a turban, and some substance for staining his face and hands a dark hue. He prepared Mrs. Ebbitt to expect a visitor. Entering his study, he spent a long time undressing and dressing himself in his new suit, staining his face and hands (there were several Oriental mirrors in the study which would come in useful). Then he carefully arranged his garments as they would be found in a case of general de-materialisation; re-buttoning and re-tying and re-lacing. Then he packed his bag with some necessaries for travelling; took the money from the safe in the wall; put it in the bag along with his sticks of grease-paint; donned his turban; picked up his new umbrella; surveyed his appearance in the mirror, and slipping out of the French window knocked at the hall-door.

"He completely deceived Mrs. Ebbitt as to his identity; yet she realised that his figure was familiar. When she had gone into the dining-room, he opened the study door, and, by speaking loudly in Hindustani and English, alternately, he created the illusion of two persons engaged in conversation. There was no need for him to speak in English at all, except to give an ignorant listener that impression; for Danvers spoke Hindustani like a native. He knew also that the word 'Bombay' would stick in her memory, and that she would repeat it to the genuine messenger from Bombay despatched by the society; in which case the latter would think that he had been forestalled, and by the time he had made inquiries Danvers would be far away. Later on, he carried out a similar dialogue in two languages for the benefit of the housekeeper, when he apologised for not showing his guest to the door. When Mrs. Ebbitt had closed the hall-door on the 'visitor', he went round and entered the study by the window, picked up his bag, and left the house noiselessly.

"Where he went, still disguised as a Hindu lawyer, or where he abandoned the disguise for another, or how he got away from England, I cannot tell—though I might invent twenty different theories. The fact remains that he must have sailed for South America. Anyway, I learnt last year from a member of the Oriental Society that the editor of the society's journal was the recipient of a very learned critique upon an article which appeared in the issue of the previous quarter. It was undated and unsigned, but the envelope bore the postage stamps of Ecuador. So, I presume that Danvers is still living in disguise, or that Ecuador is one of those few bright spots where emissaries from the Swastika-Prabandh cease from troubling."

The Rejuvenation
of Ivan Smithovitch

Since the Russification of England by the Bolsheviks, I hear that English speakers have now the proverbial life of a dog. The misguided individual who would venture to utter a word of English in Piccadillsky or the Strandskaya, at the present time, would get a bullet through him before he could say Jacksky Robinsonovitch; and everyone knows that the true Anglo-Saxon likes to breathe that pious aspiration in moments of peril. In a way I pity the unfortunate Sassenachs; although there was a period when they proscribed the Irish language in this country; but the Nemesis which has overtaken them would move a heart of stone.

I was just pondering over their evil plight when who should drop in but my old friend John Smith—Ivan Smithovitch, I mean. I am always afraid for my life that the words will slip out from me involuntarily when I am on a visit to his place, he has a nice house on the Thamesky Prospect. Ivan, I may as well explain, was the founder of the Society for the Preservation of Cockney English; and he often consulted me as to the best methods to adopt. He speaks Irish fluently, but with an atrocious Cockney accent. Well, who should drop in but Ivan? I scarcely recognised him. He had lost the appearance of decrepitude which had stolen over his form during the last few years. His face was fresh; his voice rang clear; and his hand-grip was vigorous.

"How are you, my dear fellow?" he said. "I'm delighted to see you. It's a long time since we met." He spoke in Irish, the peculiarities of which I cannot represent in English.

"Yes," I agreed, "and the effect of the long absence is quite evident in your Gaelic, which is, if possible, worse than it was twenty years ago. You ought to spend six months at least in Donegal. But sit down, old man, and light up. Whisper! What do you say to a glass of beer?"

"Beer!" he explained. "Beer! It is tears and not beers that are flowing in my country, of late. I'd give a guinea for a bottle of Gwynne's Twenty."

"You mean Guinness's XX," I corrected; "I have two in the cupboard here, camouflaged as a pair of field-glasses." I opened a bottle and poured it out for him. He drained it at a draught.

"A thousand thanks," he said; "I needed that."

"A drink precedes a story," said I, "according to the Gaelic proverb. Now that you have 'wet your mouth and your body inside', like the Yellow Bittern in the old song, tell me what has brought you here?"

"The last time I was here," he replied, "I told you from beginning to end the history of the English Language Movement since the day the Russians first took possession of my ill-starred land. We did our best to keep our language alive; but we failed miserably. English is dying out fast; and no wonder, considering the forces that have been brought to bear against us. There are only six people in the City of London who can speak English; and with the lapse of time it is probable that ten years hence we six shall have passed away. The possibility has weighed much upon my mind, and I have been racking my brains to devise some plan for prolonging the life of our poor language. At last, after many a sleepless night spent in meditation, an idea occurred to me. You see, when I die—I'm the youngest of the six—the English language dies; I'm certain of that—"

"Splendid!" I shouted. "A glorious opportunity!" So saying, I reached for the poker and whirled it over his head, as though contemplating his immediate taking off. "When you die, Ivan Smithovitch, not only will English die, but the worst bad Gaelic ever spoken in Ireland will die also Say 'Jacksky Robinsonovitch' or as sure as I'm brandishing this poker you're done!"

Of course, I was only joking; but Ivan became terrified. He went down on his knees and begged me to spare his life until I had at least heard the rest of the story. I granted him permission to continue.

"It was all your own fault," I said, "when you let that secret slip out that your death would mean the death of English—not to mention Bad Irish. But proceed."

He sat down in his chair again, and wiped his forehead, for the cold perspiration was running down his face. I poured out the second bottle of stout and handed it to him. Once more he drained the glass at a draught, sighed, and continued his narrative.

"When I realised that English would die with me, it appeared to me to be my patriotic duty to live as long as possible. I saw an advertisement, in a German paper, which stated that a clever specialist was prepared to carry out the operation of monkey-gland grafting on a limited number of men over sixty, gratis, in order to test a new experiment. I went to Germany, and had the operation performed. In a fortnight's time I was walking about the streets again. In a month's time I noticed that I was growing more vigorous in every way. I found that I could walk and run like a youth; but there was something wrong about the monkey-gland; for I experience a tremendous longing for climbing. It is as much as I can do to pass a tree without leaping on to a branch and swinging there. My earnest prayer is that I do not grow a tail in the end of my days. It's a sorrowful story, isn't it?" and then he began to chatter like an ape.

"Yes," said I, "Kipling, the last of the English poets, was right:

> *"That is the sorrowful story that they tell*
> *when the twilight fails,*
> *And the monkeys walk together,*
> *holding each other's tails."*

I seized the poker once more, to poke the fire; but poor Ivan thought I was going to attack him in earnest. He screeched loudly, leaped up to the curtain-pole, and out he went through the window, which was open at the top. He climbed on to the roof, and walked across some telephone wires till he reached the houses on the opposite side of the street. Then he stopped. I shouted to him at the top of my voice

"What on earth has come over you?" I yelled. "You certainly have got a double dose of monkeyness. You nearly broke your own neck crossing over by those wires a moment ago; and in that case you would have broken English in addition to your already broken Irish! Come back, man alive; I didn't intend the poker for you at all!"

All he did was gibber at me like an ape; and when he began to hurl pieces of broken slates at me from the roof of the house on which he was standing, my pity changed to disgust. I dived in for the two empty bottles, and returned armed with them.

"Look out, you wretch!" I shouted. "Shame on you! You have acquired the ill manners as well as the youth of monkeydom. May the Bolsheviks catch you!"

I sent the two bottles hurtling at him across the street, and they broke into smithereens against the roof opposite. Ivan dodged from roof to roof until he disappeared from sight. That is how my friend, Ivan Smithovitch, became rejuvenated; and that is how I lost him. I don't suppose I shall ever see him again; or if I do it will be in the London Zoölogisky Sadi (Gardens) I shall see him. Somehow I feel that the old Ivan I knew is dead; as dead as Chaucerian English; and I have not the slightest desire to hear broken Irish chattered by any denizen of the Monkey House in London or elsewhere.

Selected Essays

Dream Stuff

The experiments of psychologists, like Maury, Simon, and Tissie in France, Scherner in Germany, and more recently of Professor Ladd in America, have thrown considerable amount of light on the "stuff that dreams are made on". It has been conclusively shown that in most instances the starting-point of a dream is a simple sensation of sight, sound, or touch. The mention of sight is enough to invite scepticism at the outset, yet Bergson states emphatically, that our dreams are mostly visual: "Sounds do not hold so great a place in most dreams as shapes and colours. Often, indeed, we are only seeing when we believe ourselves to be also hearing." M. Max Simon observes that sometimes it happens that we are dreaming we are engaged in a conversation, and then suddenly we become aware that no one is speaking, and that no one has spoken: between our interlocutor and ourself a direct interchange of thought was going on, a silent conversation. A strange phenomenon, yet easy to explain. To hear sounds in a dream, it is generally necessary that real sounds should be perceived. Out of nothing the dream can make nothing. What is it, then, that we see in our visions? What is going on when we close our eyes? "Most people," replies Bergson, "would say there is nothing going on. That is because they are not carefully attending. First, there is a black background. Then appear colour blotches, sometimes dull, sometimes of singular brilliancy. These spots spread and shrink, changing form and tone, constantly shifting." Physiologists and psychologists have described this phenomenon as "light-dust" or "phosphenes", and attributed the appearances to the slight modifications which are ceaselessly taking place in the circulation of the blood in the retina, or to the pressure which the closed lid exerts upon the eyeball, causing a mechanical excitation of the optic nerve; but whatever be the explanation of the phenomena or the name by which they are called, the fact remains that they are the colours on the palette which the dream-artist employs to paint his picture.

Professor Ladd found that by keeping the eyes closed on awakening, and retaining for some moments the dream about to take flight, he could see the objects of the dream dissolve into the coloured spots which the eye really perceived when the lids were closed. But apart from this subjective source of vision there are visual sensations which reach us from external causes. Even with the eyelids closed we can still distinguish light from shade, and even, to a certain extent, recognise the nature of the light; and the sensations evoked by the stimulus of a light suddenly falling upon the closed lids will produce a variety of dreams dominated by the idea of fire. Thus, one dreamer imagined that he was present at a fire in three different places in quick succession—at a theatre, a public square, and the Paris Exhibition; while another dreamer, who had served in the Navy, dreamed that he was on a voyage, during which there were lightning flashes, and afterwards a battle, in which he saw the fire belching from the mouths of the guns. When they woke up they discovered that the light in each case was the beam thrown by the dark lantern which the hospital nurse going her round had flashed toward the bed in passing.

As for sounds, there are internal sounds to which we are deaf while awake, but which we may clearly distinguish in sleep; the throb of pulsating arteries, and sensations of buzzing, tinkling, and whistling in the ear itself, sometimes exaggerated in the case of aural disease, yet always present to some degree, but passing unnoticed in the hubbub of louder external sounds that assail our ears in waking, just as we are unconscious of the "light-dust" until our attention is directed to it. There are also external sounds which we may continue to hear after we have fallen asleep, such as the creaking of chairs, the rain beating against the window, or the wind playing its chromatic scale in the chimney. Bergson records an amusing dream of his own caused by an external sound. He dreamt that he was on a platform addressing an assembly. A confused murmur arose in the back of the auditorium. It increased to a frightful uproar. At length the whole audience seemed to be on their feet shouting in regular rhythm, "Out! Out!" Then he awoke to find that a dog was barking in a neighbouring garden, and that it was the rhythmic "Wow! Wow!" of the dog that supplied the "Out! Out!" of his dream, and it was to account for the disagreeable sound that his dream-self evolved the *mise-en-scène* of the lecture-hall.

The curious thing about the process is that the dream seems to work backward from what was really the starting-point, so as to write an introduction to it. The common dream-experience of flying, floating, or moving through space without touching the ground is explained as resulting from a combination of two circumstances. The dreamer retains so much of his waking tactile sensations that he is conscious of the fact that his feet are not touching the ground, for the simple reason that he is lying down in bed; but at the same time in his dream he is standing up and walking about; therefore he feels that he is moving through space free from the law of gravitation.

Sleeplessness

Of all the fiendish refinements of torture evolved by Chinese ingenuity, the forcible prevention of sleep occupies the foremost rank; but, after all, the wretched victim could sleep if only he were permitted to do so. It is the irony of fate that the sufferer from insomnia, on the most comfortable of couches, and with twelve hours' rest at his disposal, woos sleep in vain. Sleeplessness is the bane of modern civilisation, and the number of persons who must perforce choose between the two evils of a sleepless night or recourse to drugs has reached an alarming percentage.

We may derive some small modicum of comfort from the reflection that causes of insomnia are definitely known. Excluding cases of mental disorder or physical pain, dyspepsia, worry, and nervous excitement account for most instances of sleeplessness, and, naturally, worry is the cause least easily removed. A burdened conscience banishes sleep just as effectually as the Chinese torturer. The Ancient Mariner, in Coleridge's poem, is afflicted with insomnia as a punishment for slaying the albatross. Lady Macbeth suffers from two disorders of sleep—somnambulism and somniloquism, walking and talking in her sleep. Her partner in crime is so tormented by fearful visions that he is afraid to sleep "In the affliction of these terrible dreams that shake us nightly."

We can produce dreams artificially—for example, by uncovering the feet of a sleeper we make him dream that he is walking in water; but over the natural "frightfulness" of self-evolved dreams we have no control, as Elizabeth Barrett Browning so pathetically complains:

"Sleep, soft, beloved!" we sometimes say;
But have no tune to charm away
Sad dreams that through the eye-lids creep."

But the confirmed insomniac would cheerfully risk "what dreams may come" in exchange for the certainty of dropping off to sleep within a reasonable time after retiring to rest.

Many and various are the subterfuges to which the sufferer has recourse in order to court the favour of the god, Morpheus: counting imaginary sheep, as they pass one by one through an imaginary gap, or leap over an imaginary fence; conjuring up a monotony of sound, or forming mental pictures of placid expanses of land or sea. Yet there are nights when each and all of these time-honoured devices fail signally, as Wordsworth knew by bitter experience:

"A flock of sheep that leisurely pass by
One after one: the sound of rain, and bees
Murmuring; the fall of rivers, winds, and seas,
Smooth fields, white sheets of water, and pure sky;—
I've thought of all by turns, and still I lie
Sleepless."

Possibly we should solve the problem if we could discover the cause of sleep; a cause which is still unknown. Physiologists are wont to conceal their ignorance in a cloud of verbiage. What, for example, is the good of informing us that "it is probably associated with the great cosmical alternation of day and night, and with the diminished molecular activity that takes place in the cerebral cell"? That's the stuff to give Einstein. Some have it that sleep is a form of blood-poisoning, due to auto-intoxication resulting from the absorption into the system of exhaustion-products. But said Claparède of Geneva, if that is so, how comes it that new-born infants who take no exercise sleep a great deal; while old persons, who are easily wearied and exhausted, sleep little? On the contrary, he said, we sleep to prevent ourselves becoming exhausted.

Of course, the dreaded "sleepy sickness" is caused by the intoxication produced by the poison of a microscopic parasite called the trypanosome, or "gimlet-bodied" creature; but auto-intoxication will not explain the sleeping-sickness which seizes so many occupants of pews during a prosy sermon! No; the secret of "Nature's soft nurse" continues to baffle the prying investigations of the world's greatest scientists, just as successfully as it baffles the ordinary humble citizen who cannot sleep.

The Nervous Child

The heart of Charles Dickens would have rejoiced to see the day when the neurotic child, instead of being treated with the greatest cruelty as an unmitigated nuisance, has come to be regarded as a possession to be treasured. Medical men and professors of education have taken up his cause and pleaded it with an earnestness which is certain to bear good fruit. The neurotic child, we are assured, is not a diseased child, he is the stuff of which great men are made—of such is the kingdom of genius.

It is pathetic to read the childish experiences of Dickens, with all the phobias which obsessed him; for *David Copperfield* and *Great Expectations*, and some chapters in *Dombey and Son* are but thinly-disguised autobiographies. To a nervous child, the life at one of the public schools of Dickens' day must have proved a torture chamber, fitted with more ingenious contrivances and methods for the infliction of acute physical and mental agony than any that ever graced the dungeons of the Spanish inquisition. Not that home-life would necessarily be a bed of roses for a boy of such disposition. The thoughtless and unfeeling adult, with nerves of steel, cannot avoid giving a constant succession of shocks, quite unintentionally, to the child whose nerves are so highly-strung that they are perpetually a-quiver with emotions that pass the bovine-natured by. His nervous system is like the "aerial" of a wireless station, with a receiver tuned up to catch the faintest and most distant ripple in the ether of thought. The normal child will listen with interest to the story of the raising of Lazarus, and will probably not experience any stronger emotion than one of curiosity, mingled with a certain regret that there is no possibility of his witnessing a similar event. Not so with David Copperfield, when his mother read the story one Sunday night to Peggotty and him: "I am so frightened that they are afterwards obliged to take me out of bed, and show me the quiet churchyard out of the bedroom window, with the dead all lying in their graves at rest, below the solemn moon." Children, as Macaulay says, are of all persons the most imaginative, and it is in nervous ones that imagination runs riot; but the demon is not to be exorcised by enforced study, as Miss Murdstone held: "Clara, my dear, there's nothing like work; give your boy an exercise." Exercise—not an exercise—was what poor Davy most needed; but here, again, the self-opinionated martinet interfered, with evil results. "As to any recreation with other children of my own age I had very little of that, for the gloomy theology of the Murdstones made all children out to be a swarm of little vipers (though there was a child once set in the midst of the disciples), and held that they contaminated one another. The natural result of this treatment was to make me sullen, dull, and dogged." Again, to boys of the Tommy Traddles type, the sternest schoolmaster that ever wielded a cane is only a passing memory, a figure that mellows with the years, and that even assumes somewhat of a halo when viewed from the standpoint of a middle-aged pater familias; but it is not so much the cane of the ruler that David dreads so much as the omnipresent feeling of repression which clings to him even outside school-hours. "Here am I in the playground with my eye still fascinated by him (Mr. Creakle), though I can't see him. The window, at a little distance from which I know he is having his dinner, stands for him, and I eye that instead. If he shows his face near it, mine assumes an imploring and submissive expression." There are few more pathetic pictures in literature than that of poor little Paul Dombey, seated in Dr. Blimber's study, listening to the solemn ticking of the big clock, which seems to say "How—is—my—little—friend?" The crime of setting a little soul to construe Cornelius Nepos, when all he wants to know is "What are the waves saying?" Southey, the poet, was another example of the man of genius grown from a delicate neurotic plant. A failure at school, from which he was expelled for writing an essay on the subject of "Flogging" in the school magazine, he was refused admission at Christ Church, Oxford, for the same reason; and the indefinable fears or phobias of childhood clung to him in manhood, and unfitted him for the learned professions. He was scared from the Church by dogma, from medicine by the dissecting-room, and from law by dullness, but he made good as a poet. His early experiences he sums up in a single sad line:

"The days of childhood are but days of woe."

Another pathetic picture, which is withal somewhat tinged with humour, is that of the child Handel—also a neurotic child, who went into convulsions at the sound of a trumpet—practising the forbidden art of music on the old spinet, which a good-natured aunt had smuggled into the attic, where its sound might not reach the lower part of the house; for his father despised art, and had destined him for the law.

But the day of repression and unsympathetic bullying is gone. Neurotic children are no longer to be left to the tender mercies of unimaginative nurses who terrify them into silence, if not to sleep, by stories of horrible bogies, raw-heads, and bloody-bones. The fear of the dark is recognised by Bacon as being as instinctive in children as the fear of death is in adults; and wise parents will not grudge a night-light if all other methods of reasoning with a dread which is essentially unreasonable, just because it is instinctive and primitive, prove unavailing. So also, with the peculiar antics and habits, the nervous twitching and gestures which in children of this particular diathesis are so irritating to phlegmatic adults. Scolding is no remedy. On the contrary, it makes matters a thousand times worse. The wiser plan is to ignore completely such manifestations; and they will disappear in time, when the nervous energy which bubbles over through these curious outlets finds itself directed into definite channels of utility.

It must be remembered that, from the psychological point of view, there is nothing more harmful than the production of artificial complexes to check impulses which are already suffering from the effects of repression due to environment. The Decalogue is sometimes more than adults can bear. To add to it daily a new series of enactments in the shape of "Thou shalt not's" is to place a crushing burden upon the shoulders of the young. Patience will bring its own reward. Let the sorely-tried parent or teacher reflect that genius hath somewhat of the infantine, and genius is always eccentric.

The Language of the Future

The story of the abortive attempt to build the Tower of Babel bears witness to the fact that early in the history of the human race polyglottism was regarded as a curse and a hindrance, that it is still so regarded is evidenced by the numerous endeavours which have been made within the last three hundred years to construct an artificial international language. In the opinion of the Biblical writer of the Golden Age obtained when "the whole earth was of one language and of one speech"; and practical people of all nations at the present day hold that a return to monoglottism is a consummation devoutly to be wished. As compared with natural languages, artificial tongues are a delicate and sickly brood. The number of naturally evolved languages (known to philological science) which have died without issue may be reckoned on fingers of both hands; whereas the "Strangers' Plot" in the linguistic cemetery already bristles with tombstones of artificial weaklings and monstrosities. Since the appearance in 1653 of "Logopandekteision, or an introduction to the Universal Language, digested into six several books by Sir Thomas Urquart, of Cromartie, Knight", the monoglot movement has given birth to close on seventy artificial tongues. Of these some were stillborn, others through lack of skilled attention succumbed shortly after birth; others still bore within their systems the seeds of impracticability, a malady which carried them off in the space of a few years. Esperanto, the most famous product since the late lamented Volapuk, has maintained its existence only by exacting from its devotees an unquestioning obedience to official authority, and an act of faith in the inadmissibility of change (even for the better). But already there are symptoms of a rift within the lute; even among the closely-herded ranks of the "*samideanoj*" there are those who claim the right of private judgement, and a reformed Esperanto is now well on its way. Meantime, while manufactured lingoes are being born to trouble and inevitable extinction as the sparks fly upwards, natural evolution, by means of the law of the survival of the fittest, is working steadily towards the desired goal. If the present rate of progress be maintained—and everything points to its acceleration rather than its retardation—English, already the language of the British Isles, North America, Australia, New Zealand, and part of Africa, will in another hundred years be the official language of Mexico, Brazil, and the greater part of Africa; while it will have replaced Hindustani as the inter-tribal speech of all India. English-speaking missionaries will have familiarised all Heathendom with its sound, and it will be taught as an essential subject in the schools of China and Japan, as well as those in Europe. By the year 3000 AD three-eighths of the world's population will be English-speaking monoglots, and the remaining five-eighths bilinguists and polyglots having English as one of their languages.

This will mean that the battle will be practically won because one language, English, will be understood all the world over. Still the earth will even at this stage, be far from being of one language and of one speech.

The descendants of the Romance, Teutonic, and Slavonic tongues of to-day will cling tenaciously to parts of Europe and Siberia; a bastard Arabic will still be heard in Arabia, Syria, and Africa; while Chinese, which by this time will have become once more inflexional, will be the home language of the East. The final struggle for survival will be between English and Chinese, and the struggle will end by English borrowing and assimilating all the most useful terms and expressions in Chinese and leaving residue to die of disuse. We may assume that about the year 6000 AD the whole earth will be of one speech, and that speech English. It will be a language of very remarkable uniformity as regards pronunciation, accent, and idiom; for the marvellous facilities for travel in those days, and the hourly publication and interchange of news from all capitals and great centres by telephonogram, will render dialects and local peculiarities short-lived. The language of the future will be English but it will not be English of Shakespeare or Milton or Ruskin. It will be the legitimate descendent of the English used at the present day in ordinary conversation; not the language of the pulpit, or the platform, or the Press; and it will be a very much modified, simplified and apocopated English. The language of every-day life of the business firm, the bank the Stock Exchange will be purely monosyllabic; while the poet, the scientist, and the divine will occasionally employ archaic or technical forms of two or more syllables. The far-reaching influence of the bustling go-ahead people of Yang-Lan (*i.e.* Yank-land; *i.e.* America) will have contributed largely to this result, as against the more conservative instincts of Ying-Lan (*i.e.* England) and of some portions of the Brit-emp (British Empire). That such a dogmatic forecast is not an abuse of the liberty of prophesying will be clear from the following considerations.

It is the law of nature that all continuous forces take the line of least resistance. The forces of progress find the English language the easiest method of escape from the impasse of polyglottism. Apart altogether from the question of its present system of orthography, English is destined to be the language of the future owing to three unique advantages, *viz.*, (1) its numberless, genderless, indeclinable definite article; (2) the absence of distinctions of gender in verb, noun, adjective, and participle; (3) its steadily increasing tendency towards ultimate monosyllabism. Taking these points in order, it is obvious that a definite article is an indispensable adjunct to a language which hopes to survive and to remain the medium for the expression of accurate thought, accordingly the Slavonic tongues may at once be put out of court. Again, how can the German with its "*der, die, das, des, dem, den*", or any of the Romance languages with their "*le, la, les, il, la, lo, i, le, el, los, las, o, a, os, as*", hope to compete with the unvarying English: the English, like Chinese, has long since abolished distinctions of gender. Masculine, feminine, and neuter, say the grammars of other languages, the feminine forms of all parts of speech coming second. Not only so but the tyranny of these tongues compels the woman to brand herself with grammatical infamy every time she opens her mouth. An absinthe-sodden "Apache" may say "*Je suis heureux*", whereas the most emancipated Frenchwoman must proclaim her inferiority to the world by saying, "*Je suis heureuse*". When the woman adopts the English language she meets man on a plane of grammatical equality.

In conclusion, the careful observer must notice the increase of monosyllabism. It is only the witty politician who can afford to indulge in such sesquipedalian words as "terminological inexactitude" to describe what the man in the street prefers to express in two sharp syllables. "Bike, car, wire, 'phone", in business English; "soph, hols, vac, bugs, and weeds", the student's equivalents for sophister, holidays, vacation, botany, and zoölogy; the slang "cop, beak, quod, stretch, squeal", for policeman, magistrate, prison, sentence, turn King's evidence; and the "nut's" apocopations as heard in "imposs" and "posish" for impossible and position, are all straws which show clearly the direction in which the wind of development is blowing. We may feel that such a language will be more useful than beautiful and we may despair of its ever giving expression to lofty thoughts either in prose or verse; but, as a matter of fact, some of the most important and most expressive words in the language are already monosyllabic: *e.g.* God, soul, faith, love, hope, life, mind, thought, birth, death, home, wife, child, sun, moon, star, sea, land, eat, drink, wake, sleep, laugh, cry, mourn, pray, work, rest, war, peace, tomb.

Plain Smith

I well remember with what gusto the late Mir Aulad Ali, Professor of Oriental Languages in Trinity College, used to tell a story, which, if not true, is at least *ben trovato*, to the effect that an Englishman named Smith, while staying in Dublin, received an invitation to dinner from The MacDermot. The title puzzled him, but after some reflection he decided that it was a way they had in Ireland, and he wrote accepting the invitation, beginning his letter with the words: "The Smith has much pleasure in accepting the invitation of the MacDermot!"

Plain Smith, unadorned by any orthographical devices of central "y" or final "e", has come to be regarded, rightly or wrongly, as a plebian patronymic belonging to persons of ordinary red blood like the Browns, Jonses, and Robinsons, *hoc genus omne*. Yet Smith, or its equivalent in the various languages, is one of the oldest names in Europe. Old Norse "Smidr", Latin "Fabricius", Gaulish "Gobannium", Anglo-Irish "Gavin", all point back to a high antiquity and a period when Smith was an honoured name, derived from a respected profession.

I know of few more risky experiments than that of tracing one's pedigree; it is an unpleasant shock to modern susceptibilities to discover, perhaps, that one's great-great-great-granduncle's brother-in-law was executed for cattle-driving. One can only breathe with ease when one has climbed downwards to the trunk of the family tree, and we can all agree without a blush that our first parents were guilty of disobedience. This being so, I feel sure that no one of the name of Smith will be angry with me for pointing out that the first man of the name was Cain, the son of Adam. Cain, in Hebrew, means "Smith"; and later on we are told of one of his descendants, Tubal Cain, or Tubal the Smith, of whom it is said that "he was a hammerer and artificer in brass and iron".

The word "smith" means simply "worker"; and before the meaning became narrowed down it was possible for the Norse to speak of a "verse-smith" *i.e.* poet, or a "mischief-smith", while the Anglo-Saxons had a word "wonder-smith". Similarly in Latin, "*faber*", meant "maker"; and our modern word "forge" has come to us through the French from the Latin "*fabrica*", the place where the smith made things.

His importance in primitive times, as the man who made weapons, may be gauged from the fact that the Greeks had a smith-god, Hephaestus, and the Latins their Vulcan. The apotheosis of the smith, strange though it may appear to our modern minds, was due to the amazement of primitive man at the marvellous art of melting hard metal in the fire and fashioning useful implements and articles of value out of it. The invention was consequently ascribed to supernatural beings, and further, the exercise of the art by mortal beings could not be conceived without the assistance of mysterious and magical means. The result of the latter mode of reasoning was that the smith became gradually associated with the *black arts*, more especially as he was also the surgeon and general practitioner of the community, much as the barber of a later day included blood-letting in the list of his accomplishments. I am not given to sarcasm, but men who have their beards shaved at the barber's are of opinion that the hereditary by-practice is by no means obsolete.

People in the South and West of Ireland are familiar with the blacksmith in the role of bone-setter; and I knew personally one country smith who had gained a great reputation as an amateur dentist. His *modus operandi* was as follows. A "wax-end" was firmly tied round the neck of the offending molar and the other end of the string was fastened to the anvil; then a white-hot horse-shoe, which had been secretly in readiness, was suddenly whisked out in the tongs and held under the patient's nose. The patient instinctively jerked away his head—and left his tooth behind. I never submitted to having a tooth extracted by that method, but I was assured by others that the surprise occasioned by the sudden appearance of the glowing iron in close proximity to his face, caused the patient to forget all about the pain of the extraction, or even rendered him unconscious of it.

There have been many men of the name famous and infamous, from Adam Smith, the great economist, to Joseph Smith, the founder of the Mormons; but for Irishmen who love their country there is one Smith of revered memory— Canon Sydney Smith, Anglican divine, writer and orator, whose ardent speeches in the cause of tolerance at the time of Catholic Emancipation should never be forgotten.

Ptenanthropic Warfare

"There is no new thing under the sun," says the Wise Man; and certainly the idea, if not the fact, of aviation has nothing novel about it. Ancient literature is full of allusions to flying men. Virgil, in the Sixth Book of the *Aeneid*, sings of how Daedalus, in his successful flights from Crete to Cumae on the shores of Italy, "dared to entrust himself to the air on swift wings, and glided forth to the frozen North by an unusual route, and where he first landed he dedicated the oarage of his wings to Phoebus." Silius Italicus mentions the consternation produced among fowls of the air by the appearance of the birdman; and Ovid, in his *Metamorphoses*, tells how Daedalus' son Icarus, in trying to break the record for high-flying, flew too near the sun, which melted the wax fastenings of his wings, with the result that the daring aviator found a watery grave in the Icarian Sea. Horace exclaims in pious horror—

> *"Daring all, their goal to win,*
> *Men tread forbidden ground, and rush on sin.*
> *Daedalus the void air tried*
> *On wings to human kind by Heaven denied:*
> *Nought is there for man too high;*
> *Our impious folly e'en would climb the sky."*

The first mention of a "Zeppelin" in history is contained in the Book of Leinster, where the appearance of three ships in the air is mentioned as one of the wonders of Teltown, when the King Domhnall Mc Murchadha (763 AD) was at the Fair. In the Irish Nennius there is a more circumstantial account of an airship's appearance at Teltown: "Congalach, son of Maelmithig (956 AD) was at the fair at Teltown on a certain day, when he saw a ship sailing along in the air. One of the crew cast a dart at a salmon. The dart fell down in the presence of the gathering, and a man came out of the ship after it. When he seized its end from above, a man from below seized it from below. Upon which, the man from above said: 'I am being drowned.' 'Let him go!' said Congalach; and he is allowed to go up, and then he goes from the swimming."

As a story never loses in its travels, we find a version in a still more expanded form in the Irish Mirabilia in the *Norse Speculum Regale* (circa 1250 AD): "Another thing that will seem most wonderful happened in the city of Clonmacnoise. In that city is a church which is sacred to the memory of the holy man called Kiaranus (St. Ciaran). And there it thus befell on a Sunday, when the people were at church hearing Mass, there came dropping from the air above an anchor, as if it were cast from a ship, for there was a rope attached to it. And the fluke of the anchor got hooked in an arch at the church door, and all the people went out of the church and wondered, and looked upwards after the rope. They saw a ship float on the rope and men in it. And next they saw a man leap overboard from the ship, and dive down towards the anchor, wanting to loosen it. His exertion seemed to them, by the movements of his hands and feet, like that of a man swimming in the sea. And when he came down to the anchor he endeavoured to loosen it. And then some men ran towards him and wanted to seize him. But in the church to which the anchor was fashioned there is a Bishop's Chair. The Bishop was by chance on the spot, and he forbade the men to hold the man, for he said that he would die as if he were held in water. And as soon as he was free he hastened his way up again to the ship; and as soon as he came up, they cut the rope, and then sailed on their way out of sight of men. And the anchor has ever since lain as a witness of the event in that church." So far there is no mention of warlike flying men, but we find at least the germ of the "War in the Air" theory in Plautus' comedy *Poenulus, or the Young Carthaginian*. In Act II, the following dialogue occurs:—

> *Anthemonides*—So, as I began to tell you, about the Ptenanthropic Battle [Ptenanthropos is Greek for "flying-man"] in which, with my own hands, in one day, I killed sixty thousand flying men—
> *Lycus*. What! Flying-men!
> *Anth*. Exactly. That's what I say.
> *Lycus*. Prithee, are there anywhere men that fly?
> *Anth*. There were; but I killed them.
> *Lycus*. How did you manage it?
> *Anth*. I'll tell you. I gave bird-lime and sling to my troops; beneath it they laid leaves of colts-foot.
> *Lycus*. For what?
> *Anth*. So that the bird-lime might not stick to the slings.
> *Lycus*. Go on. (*Aside*) 'Faith you lie most egregiously. (Aloud) What then?
> *Anth*. They put rather large pellets of bird-lime in their slings; they were commanded to sling with it at the enemy as they flew. To make a long story short, they hit every one with the bird-lime, and they fell to the ground as thick as pears. As each one dropped, I immediately pierced him through the brain with his own feathers, just like a turtle dove!"

Substitute airmen for flying men, bullet for pellets, and anti-aircraft guns for slings; retain a certain amount of exaggeration, and we have a yarn such as an octogenarian old soldier may yet tell to his grandchildren about his exploits during the great European War. So does the fertile imagination of man anticipate invention, and demonstrate that, in a sense at least, there is justification for the dictum: "There is no new thing under the sun!"

Cuchulainn and America

Everybody knows that the American continent was first discovered by an Irishman, Andy Merrigan.

The story goes that to celebrate the occasion, friend Andy, whose spelling was as shaky as Bill Stump's, carved his name on a rock, thus: "A. Merigan", and subsequent explorers called the continent by that name.

This legend, however, only applies to North America; a correspondent in a Dublin contemporary propounds the theory that a contingent of Irishmen arrived in South America long before the days of Columbus.

Readers of Longfellow's poem, "Hiawatha", are familiar with the North American Indian legend of the semi-divine hero who, after teaching his people the arts of peace, including the smoking of the Peace-Pipe, set out in his birch canoe for the regions of the home-wind, the Islands of the Blessed, leaving behind him the "Black-Robe Chief, the Pale-Face with the cross upon his bosom", to carry on the reformation which he had begun.

A somewhat similar legend is found among the Indians of South America. The Toltecs of Mexico worshipped as their deity a being known as Quetzalcoatl, who is described as a white man with noble features, long black hair and full beard, and dressed in flowing robes. It is said in some versions that he came originally from Yucatan, and dwelt among the Toltecs for twenty years, teaching them to follow the example of his austere and virtuous life, to hate all violence and war, to offer bread as a sacrifice upon the altar instead of men or beasts, and to do penance for their sins by mortification of the body.

Like Hiawatha, too, he taught them the art of picture-writing; but he instructed them further in the use of the calendar and the work of the silversmith. At last he departed to some unknown land; according to one tradition setting sail from the Atlantic coast on the confines of Central America; but when he reached the Atlantic he sent back his companions to tell the people among whom he had dwelt that in future ages his brethren, white men and bearded like himself, would land there after travelling the sea from the sunrise, and come to rule the country.

Mexican historians relate that the Toltec nation all but perished in the eleventh century by years of drought, famine and pestilence, a few survivors only remaining in the land, while the rest migrated into Yucatan and Guatemala, where their name is commemorated in local records.

That there is a basis of reality in these traditions is shown by the fact that the word Toltecatl, originally meaning a Toltec, came to mean among the later Aztecs an artist or skilled craftsman. But it is evident also from the tradition that there must be some historical foundation for the story of Quetzalcoatl.

It is quite possible that a Christian missionary may have found his way to Mexico or South America before the eleventh century. The traditional appearance ascribed to the teacher, to whom in the course of time divine honours came to be paid, is that of an European, at all events; and the substitution of an unbloody offering for the old human sacrifices would point to the introduction of the Mass. Of course, in all cases such as this, one has to allow for a kind of backwash of modern history into the original current of tradition or legend; and it may be that a familiarity with the doctrines and sacraments of Christianity, gained since the Spanish Conquest, may have coloured the reports handed down orally from generation to generation; but with due allowance for an element of *vaticinium post eventum* there remains a residue which only the Pyrrhonist will incontinently reject.

Granted, then, that a Christian missionary did land in Yucatan, in say the ninth or tenth century; the question arises whence did he come? Whence but from Ireland?

After the voyages of St. Brendan all things are possible where Irish missionaries are concerned. I should not care to go so far as the correspondent referred to above. According to him—and he is largely quoting from articles on the subject in American publications—the Toltecs themselves were Irish. He suggests that the word "Toltec" is a corruption of the Irish "*Tuathal-techt*", meaning "Northern-arrivals" (Is Ulster to be given the credit for everything?); the accepted meaning is that of Tollanite, or inhabitant of the reed-country.

Another ingenious suggestion is that the Mayas of Central America hailed originally from Mayo!

But the crowning of the whole theory is that the suggestion that the Mayan form of the name given to the white deity of the tradition, Cukulcan, is only a corruption of the name of the Ulster hero Cuchulainn.

Now it is one of the canons of modern philology that an etymology from sound is seldom a sound etymology; and this is a case in point. The name given to this deity by the Quiches of Guatemala is Gucumatz, which will not fit in with the theory. In my opinion both forms are corruptions of Quetzalcoatl, the Toltec word.

Who then was Quetzalcoatl?

My own honest conviction in the matter is this: the name of the early missionary is not recorded in any of the books or tongues of earth. When it comes to theorising and making suggestions, I am bold enough to maintain that, in the circumstances, my suggestion is just as good as another.

It is this: the word Quetzalcoatl was never the name of any missionary; it was the name of the Faith he taught, a word that was constantly upon his lips; it is the Toltec attempt to reproduce the word "Catholic".

An Irish Dante

Father O'Hanlon has shown, in his *Lives of the Irish Saints*, that it is highly probable that the *Divina Commedia* of Dante owes much of its plan, and even of its inspiration, to early Irish "Visions". At any rate, the Irish were in that particular field many centuries before the Italian, as the "Vision of Adamnan" and the "Vision of Fursa" testify; and the natural temptation is to argue *post hoc—ergo propter hoc*.

There exists a mediaeval Irish Vision which presents an exact parallel to Dante's poem, in that it deals successively with an *Inferno*, a *Purgatorio*, and a *Paradiso*: it is called "The Vision of Merlino".

Merlino was a robber who lived in the wilds of Bohemia. "An accursed man: for he respected neither cleric nor layman, friend nor foe; but would do any evil that man or devil could devise or imagine." His dwelling was in the heart of a wood surrounded by quagmires, so that he was secure from the approach of those who might counsel him for his good or punish him for his evil doings. It happened that one day as he wandered in quest of spoil he inadvertently entered a place where a crowded congregation was listening to a sermon. Merlino also stopped to listen, and dropped on his knees like the rest, from no higher motive than "fear of being recognised and being brought to justice". And so perforce he was obliged to hear the sermon to the end. The preacher had a melodious voice, and he pictured for his hearers the delights of heaven and the rewards of the righteous, and then he turned to the darker side of the future life, and spoke of the eternal pains in store for sinners. What chiefly appealed to Merlino was the way in which the preacher referred to "robbers and those who break the law of God and covet the goods of their neighbours, and the evilness of the place prepared for them". When the sermon was over and he slipped away among the dispersing congregation, he tried to shake off the impression the preacher had made on him, and he tried above all to forget the final destination of wicked robbers. He reassured himself by the reflection that "all that the Church had said about these things was only fraud and trickery, which she imposed upon Christians, to the end that the living of the Church might be extorted from them".

Yet withal, from thenceforward there was no day nor night wherein the words of the preacher came not into his mind and recollection, and greatly troubled his soul; and thus he thought within himself that, if it were God's will, he had rather than all the good things of this world to get but one sight of hell; that he might know whether the holy man spake truly or falsely on the day of his sermon. And that thought kept constantly recurring to his mind, to the great disturbance of his soul's peace.

One day Merlino made a business appointment with a companion of his who had a similar taste for robbery, and the place where they decided to meet was at the parting of two ways. Merlino was first at the tryst, but it was not long until he saw his comrade approaching. They sat down and took counsel together as to which road they should follow, and finally they decided to go "to the city in Bohemia called Bragansa, where there was a great fair gathering together, and where they hoped to get much plunder". Just then they saw approaching a cavalcade of wealthy people, gorgeously attired. "Dear comrade," said Merlino, "dost thou know who are these approaching us on the road?"

"I do," replied his companion; "it is a great earl of this country, by name Plutando; and he has invited people to a great feast for the king and prince of this kingdom. Yonder are some of the attendants of the king going to the castle of the earl."

On the suggestion of Merlino, they joined the retinue of the nobles, intending to reap a rich harvest later on at the castle when the feast was nearly over, and the nobles had drunk themselves into a state of somnolence. As they proceeded, they saw "a crowd of poor and humble people in that way, who were obliged to leave the path; for the people of the chariots and horses, and the proud nobles would not suffer them to walk in their midst. Wherefore the poor men had to take another road full of biting thorns and sharp-pointed stones." (Merlino was destined to see those poor people later in different circumstances.) When they reached the castle they entered the court, "where Merlino thought to find wine and delight, music and merriment of every kind. But this is how he found the place: it was too wonderful and horrible for the eye to see, for the ear to hear, or for the mind of man to conceive or understand."

The unexpected entrance upon the scene is in sharp contrast to Dante's narrative. There is no warning legend, "*Lasciate ogni speranza voi ch'entrate*" ("Abandon hope all ye who enter here"), inscribed over the portals of the Irish Inferno. Yet another surprise is in store for him. "Dear comrade," said he, "what meaneth this place to which we have come? It seemeth that thou hast deceived me in bringing me hither."

"I am not he whom thou thoughtest to be with thee," said his companion, "but a spirit from the attendants of the Almighty. He hath sent me to thee, to show thee the things that were in thy mind continually, namely, a sight of Hell, and of the pains prepared for the sons of wrath: this is Hell."

The Inferno

The Heavenly Guide explains to Merlino that there are ten kingdoms in Hell, five under the power of Beelzebub and five under the power of Lucifer; and these are their names: Lake of Death, Land of Darkness, Lowest Hell, Marsh of Fire, Land of Terror, Lake that Cannot Be Filled, Land of Tribulation, Dungeon of Pain, Fire of Poison, Land of Oblivion. Moreover, there is a demon assigned to each sin, and it is his task to try to destroy the Christian, and if this demon cannot destroy the man and drag him with him to Hell, the pains prepared for the man are doubled on the demon in addition to the pains he had before. The penalties attached to the Seven Deadly Sins are graphically described: there are fiery dragons, poisonous adders, scourgings and flailings, and smiting with sledge-hammers, and hideous flames of fire. Here is the description given of the penalty for Gluttony:—

"After that, Merlino looked aside, and beheld a great lake, wherein was water the colour of gall; and the lake was called the Lake of Pain, for one single drop of water of the lake would destroy all the creatures on the surface of the earth by the bitterness of its chill. And many people were sitting therein up to their chins; and stores of pleasant victuals floating on the water before them; yet it was not in their power to taste the food. For their feet and their hands were bound in fetters of pain, and they were trying to snatch at the food with their mouths, but it availed them not" (The notion of punishment by intense cold is peculiarly Irish). Those who died in the sin of Sloth were bound by fetters on a flaming bed. One of those who were undergoing this torture said: "Alas, that I am not on earth again for one quarter of an hour." Another lost soul answered him, saying: "Thou lost soul, what profit were it for thee to be one quarter hour on earth, and then to be cast here again to thy fiery destruction?" The first speaker explained that if he were back in his human form again he would seek mercy through repentance.

"Nay," said the other, "repentance at the wrong time profits naught: it is in the time of mercy that it were right to seek mercy, and not to spurn God for the fleeting good things of the world." The conversation impressed Merlino so much that he resolved to repent while still in his human form if ever he returned safe to earth.

"Dost thou think these pains great?" asked his guide.

"I see," said Merlino, "that tongue cannot tell, pen cannot write, man's heart cannot conceive, the hundredth part of the pains that he who suffers least in Hell endures."

His guide explains that there are greater pains than those that are seen: "When they were brought to judgement, they obtained a sight of God's Heavens, he saw the glory and delight of the city . . . this is the cause wherefore the heart and breast of the sinners are fretted—the thought of the glimpse which they obtained of the Heaven they have lost." The other unseen pain is the prospect of Eternity. "Eternity is like the wheel of a chariot. As the wheel goes round, and the part that is passed returns anew, so is Eternity."

"Are the pains of some easy in comparison with the others in Hell?" asked Merlino.

"He whose pains are least," replied the guide, "has sufficient of sorrow. However, the pain of the Christian is much greater than the pain of the Heathen and non-Christian, though they break the law daily; because the Pagan and non-Christian have no knowledge: if they had they would fulfil it better."

The Purgatorio

After this, Merlino followed his Guide until he saw on the right a terrible place full of weeping, of cries, of pains and of every kind of penalty. "And some of those who were in pains there were saying, 'How long shall I be in these pains?' and others were saying, 'O loving friends on earth, it is a pity that ye neglect the offerings for our souls, that we might obtain succour and release'." Merlino, thinking that he is still in the Inferno, asked why these souls hope for release. The Guide replies that they are now looking at souls in Purgatory being purified. These souls know that they will yet find release from their pains, and that the prayers and good deeds of the righteous on earth will shorten time: "for this cause are they calling upon their friends". One of those who were in Purgatory spake, "I thought till now that God never made a lie. He promised that I should be here but five days, and here I am for five thousand years."

"Wherefore did God deceive yonder man?" asked Merlino. "God never deceived," was the reply. "But the sorrow he has suffered is so great that he thinks he has been here five thousand years. He has not yet been five days here, and when the five days are accomplished he will go to Heaven without delay."

The Paradiso

At the end of that conversation the Spirit of Wisdom went out of Purgatory and Merlino followed him. When he went outside, Merlino saw a thing more wonderful than he had seen before: a city and royal palace, very beautiful and lovelier than the eye of man could see, for thus it was: the wall and ramparts of the city were made of crystal, of topaz, of onyx, of emerald, and of every kind of precious stone, so that it was sufficient pleasure for the angels to look upon the glory of the walls of the city. And there were beautiful pure streams of water, and beautiful trees among the streams with flowers and fruits upon them. And birds of brilliant plumage on the tops of those trees, singing songs; and if the viols, lutes, organs, and instruments of music of the world were set to make harmony with them, sweeter would be the voice and sound of one single bird than all these.

Likewise, he saw many kings and princes and people, wearing the royal, glorious raiment, with a sparkling crown of pearls and gems upon the head of each; and brighter than the glorious sun was the glitter and the sparkling they made. And he saw many golden-haired, white-visaged maidens, and young children with pure, angelic faces.

"This," said his Guide, "is the Paradise of Heaven, the place where those who do the will of God are in eternal happiness. The lovely streams yonder are the water of Life: and whoso seeth that water shall never die, nor shall thirst nor hunger be upon him, nor the weight of age nor misery. The birds are the Angels of Heaven, who are ever singing melody and praising God. The kings and princes thou sawest are the poor, lowly men who left the broad way wherein went the carriages and chariots of proud, worldly men; by almsgiving, fasting, prayer, and devotions they have earned their glorious crowns in recompense for the oppression and misery they suffered. The golden-haired maidens are those whose lives were uncorrupted; and the children with angel faces are they who died after baptism and never committed any sins."

"Alas," said Merlino, "that I am not in yonder just for one hour!"

"That cannot be," said the Spirit, "for nothing entereth yonder but purity and righteousness. And now thou hast seen the things thou didst desire to see; and I shall leave thee here with a blessing; for thou art on the world once more, and do as thou wilt from now henceforth."

Then a deep mist came around Merlino, and when it lifted he found himself standing where the Spirit Guide had come to him, at the meeting of the two roads. Then he thought on his evil life and all the visions he had seen, and he repented him of his sins. "And he cast his arms and armour from him and went to a place where was a consecrated church; and there was a river hard by the church, and he went into the river, and went down on his knees there; and the water rose to his breast, and thus he remained till evening, and the air dropping snow and frost upon him." When the night came, he entered the church and lay on the ground and prayed for forgiveness; and God sent the Guide again to assure him of pardon.

"Rise, Merlino," said he: "God has heard thy prayer. And because thou hast repented and hast a true resolve not to fall into the same sins again, He hath promised to have mercy upon thee. He commandeth thee to go among the people, teaching and revealing in every place the things thou didst see." Then Merlino rose, and from that day forth throughout his life "his was a melodious voice, teaching and drawing Christians to the Almighty: till he died a holy blessed death, giving glory and perpetual thanksgiving to the Blessed Trinity."

[While Cearnach presents a characterful retelling here, a full translation of the vision was produced by his contemporary, R. A. Stewart Macalister: The Vision of Merlino: An Irish Allegory *(M. H. Gill & Son, Dublin, 1906). – Ed.]*

Sources

The Fatal Move and Other Stories
was first published by
M. H. Gill & Son (Dublin) in 1924.

‡

"Plain Smith" and "An Irish Dante"
were collected in *The Writings on the Walls*.
Dublin: M. H. Gill & Son, 1915.

"The Nervous Child", "Dream Stuff",
and "Ptenanthropic Warfare" were collected in
The Age of Whitewash. Dublin: M. H. Gill & Son, 1921.

"The Language of the Future", "Sleeplessness",
and "Cuchulainn and America" were collected in
Old Wine & New. Dublin: M. H. Gill & Son, 1922.

Acknowledgements

The publisher and editor would like to thank Rob Brown, Aislínn Clarke, Timothy J. Jarvis, Meggan Kehrli, Alison Lyons of Dublin UNESCO City of Literature, Ken Mackenzie, and Jim Rockhill for their assistance in the composition and production of this volume, the first time Conall Cearnach's *The Fatal Move* has been reprinted in nearly one hundred years.

About the Author

"Conall Cearnach" (1876-1929)—F. W. O'Connell—was a polyglot and scholar born in Clifden, Co. Galway. After serving as an Anglican priest, he became the first lecturer of Celtic Languages and Literature at Queen's University, Belfast. Interested in strange literature, O'Connell made the first translation into Irish of Robert Louis Stevenson's *Cas aduain an Dr Jekyll agus Mhr Hyáe* in 1929. O'Connell died tragically when he was struck by a bus in October of that year.

About the Editor

Reggie Chamberlain-King is a writer, musician, and archivist of the unusual. With Blackstaff Press, he has published *Weird Belfast* (2014), *Weird Dublin* (2015), and *The Black Dreams: Strange Stories from Northern Ireland* (2021). He is creative producer with Wireless Mystery Theatre and, with composer Martin White, turned E.T.A. Hoffman's *Master Flea* into a musical. His audio adaptation of Le Fanu's *Green Tea* was released by Swan River Press (2019). He is a regular contributor to BBC Radio Ulster and presents documentaries on the strange for Radio 4. He lives in Whitehead, Co. Antrim, with his wife, two dogs, and an unspecified fear.

SWAN RIVER PRESS

Founded in 2003, Swan River Press is an independent publishing company, based in Dublin, Ireland, dedicated to gothic, supernatural, and fantastic literature. We specialise in limited edition hardbacks, publishing fiction from around the world with an emphasis on Ireland's contributions to the genre.

www.swanriverpress.ie

"While small publishers often produce beautiful books, few can match those from Swan River Press."

– Washington Post

"It [is] often down to small, independent, specialist presses to keep the candle of horror fiction flickering . . . "

– The Irish Times

"Swan River Press—cutting edge of New Gothic."

– Joyce Carol Oates

"The redoubtable Brian J. Showers [keeps] the myriad voices of Irish fantasy alive there in Dublin."

– Alan Moore

EARTH-BOUND
and Other Supernatural Tales

Dorothy Macardle

Originally published in 1924, the nine tales that comprise Earth-Bound were written by Dorothy Macardle while she was held a political prisoner in Dublin's Kilmainham Gaol and Mountjoy Prison. The stories incorporate themes that intrigued her throughout her life; themes out of the myths and legends of Ireland; ghostly interventions, dreams and premonitions, clairvoyance, and the Otherworld in parallel with this one. It is so easy to dismiss them, as some have, merely as part of the narrative of "Irish nationalism" of the time, but it is the supernatural elements that make them much more. She would revisit these themes in later works such as her classic haunted house novel *The Uninvited* (1941). To this new edition of Macardle's debut collection, reprinted for the first time in ninety years, we have added four more tales of the supernatural.

"Beautifully written, with a fine air for the music of language and vivid descriptions of the landscape."

– Black Static

"A beautifully presented and valuable resource for anyone interested in Irish history, culture or literature."

– Dublin Inquirer

BENDING TO EARTH
Strange Stories by Irish Women

edited by Maria Giakaniki
and Brian J. Showers

Irish women have long produced literature of the gothic, uncanny, and supernatural. *Bending to Earth* draws together twelve such tales. While none of the authors herein were considered primarily writers of fantastical fiction during their lifetimes, they each wandered at some point in their careers into more speculative realms—some only briefly, others for lengthier stays.

Names such as Charlotte Riddell and Rosa Mulholland will already be familiar to aficionados of the eerie, while Katharine Tynan and Clotilde Graves are sure to gain new admirers. From a ghost story in the Swiss Alps to a premonition of death in the West of Ireland to strange rites in a South Pacific jungle, *Bending to Earth* showcases a diverse range of imaginative writing which spans the better part of a century.

> "Bending to Earth *is full of tales of women walled-up in rooms, of vengeful or unforgetting dead wives, of mistreated lovers, of cruel and murderous husbands.*"
>
> – Darryl Jones, *Irish Times*

> "*A surprising, extraordinary anthology featuring twelve uncanny and supernatural stories from the nineteenth century . . . highly recommended, extremely enjoyable.*"
>
> – *British Fantasy Society*

NOVEMBER NIGHT TALES

Henry C. Mercer

Each story in *November Night Tales* is a differently coloured gem whose many facets reflect the lively mind of the author. Henry C. Mercer's life-long interest in world mythology, fairy tales, local legend, symbols, and artifacts form the fabric of his tales. Here, the reader will find vanishing castles, secret sects, biological weapons, sinister wilderness, lycanthropy, possessed dolls, and mythical lands. The characters in each story are driven to explore the unknown, face their fears, and perhaps discover something of themselves in the process. The compelling narratives, infused with intelligence and humanity, leave the reader curious why the stories remain virtually unknown today, and mournful that there are not more to explore. United at last with the six original November night tales is a seventh, posthumously published story, *The Well of Monte Corbo*. First published in 1928, this new edition is fully illustrated by Alisdair Wood and features an introduction by Peter Bell.

> *"While they might be over ninety years old, the tales feel fresh and modern in the way they address genre sensibilities, and Swan River are to be thanked for bringing this intriguing work back into print."*

> *– Black Static*

> *"The stories cover a wide range of themes exploring the various sides of dark fiction and displaying Mercer's many faces as a writer . . . a pleasant re-discovery of a neglected little gem from a not too distant past."*

> *– Mario Guslandi*

www.ingramcontent.com/pod-product-compliance
Lightning Source LLC
Chambersburg PA
CBHW021716190726
48289CB00008B/2558